She took a deep breath, forcing herself to be honest, hating the words she knew she'd have to say if she was ever going to let anyone in. 'I can't have children, Luke.'

And she waited. For what, she didn't know—disappointment, perhaps?

'I'm sorry,' Luke said, 'for the pain that must have caused you.'

Molly gulped. 'You don't mind?'

'Mind?' Luke frowned at her question. 'I mind because I love you—I mind because it's something you clearly want. But you're asking if I mind like it's some sticking point in a contract. I love you!' Luke continued, and as he said it he stared right into her heart, peeled off that last little piece of shell around it with his eyes. 'All of you. Even that bit of you that can't have kids yet somehow manages to love working with them...and especially that bit of you that would consider loving mine?'

There was a very big question mark at the end of it.

'I love you too…' Molly answered. 'All three of you!'

Carol Marinelli recently filled in a form where she was asked for her job title and was thrilled, after all these years, to be able to put down her answer as 'writer'. Then it asked what Carol did for relaxation and after chewing her pen for a moment Carol put down the truth—'writing'. The third question asked—'What are your hobbies?' Well, not wanting to look obsessed or, worse still, boring, she crossed the fingers on her free hand and answered 'swimming and tennis'. But—given that the chlorine in the pool does terrible things to her highlights, and the closest she's got to a tennis racket in the last couple of years is watching the Australian Open—I'm sure you can guess the real answer!

Recent titles by the same author:

Medical™ Romance
BILLIONAIRE PRINCE, ORDINARY NURSE*
THE SINGLE DAD'S MARRIAGE WISH
NEEDED: FULL-TIME FATHER

Modern™ Romance
ITALIAN BOSS, RUTHLESS REVENGE
EXPECTING HIS LOVE-CHILD*
BOUGHT BY THE BILLIONAIRE PRINCE†

**The House of Kolovsky*
†*The Royal House of Niroli*

A DOCTOR, A NURSE: A LITTLE MIRACLE

BY
CAROL MARINELLI

MILLS & BOON®
Pure reading pleasure™

All the characters in this book have no existence outside the imagination of the author, and have no relation whatsoever to anyone bearing the same name or names. They are not even distantly inspired by any individual known or unknown to the author, and all the incidents are pure invention.

First published in Great Britain 2008
Large Print edition 2009
Harlequin Mills & Boon Limited,
Eton House, 18-24 Paradise Road,
Richmond, Surrey TW9 1SR

ISBN: 978 0 263 20497 1

Set in Times Roman 16½ on 20 pt.
17-0309-47098

Printed and bound in Great Britain
by CPI Antony Rowe, Chippenham, Wiltshire

A DOCTOR,
A NURSE:
A LITTLE MIRACLE

For Marilyn, Jo, Delia and Kathryn—
This dedication is for you!
Carol xxx

CHAPTER ONE

'HI, MOLLY!'

Head down, bottom up in the IV drawer certainly wasn't the way Molly had envisaged meeting Luke again.

Years ago, she'd sworn that if their paths should ever cross again she'd be thin, thin, thin, and wearing some strappy little black number, with her wild curly brown hair for once all sleek and straightened, sipping champagne—at a party, perhaps, with a gorgeous, *doting* man on her arm, laughing together at some intimate joke…. Oh, and she'd frown, just a tiny little frown as, for a second or two, she tried to place him…

'Oh, hi, Luke!'

Blushing, pulling down her top to cover her

less-than-skinny bottom as she stood, Molly managed not one of the above aims.

She'd heard he was back in Melbourne—had heard the terrible news about his wife, and had sort of wondered if he'd come back to Melbourne Central—but really her mind had been too full of other things to dwell on it.

'How are you, Molly?' His voice was as deep as ever and he looked the same—sort of.

Still taller than most, still blonder than most, those green eyes still gorgeous and that voice still incredibly crisp—only he looked older.

Not fat, balding, beer-gut older.

Just…her chocolate-brown eyes scrutinised his face for a second before she answered…tired, Molly almost decided, then changed her mind. Sad, perhaps, but that didn't quite fit either.

'I'm well, thanks.' So much for some sparkling, witty reply! 'And you?'

'Not bad.'

Of all the stupid questions to ask. Molly could have kicked herself, but instead she took a deep breath and tried to repeat the words she'd offered in the card she'd sent him six months ago.

'I was so sorry to hear…' Her voice faltered. It was easier to write it than say it. On second thoughts, even writing it hadn't been that easy—it had taken five cards and about a week of drafts to come up with her rather paltry offering.

Dear Luke,

I heard the terrible news about Amanda at work.

I am so sorry for your loss.

So sorry for the twins' loss, too.

Am thinking of you all.

Molly (Hampton née Jones, Children's Ward at Melbourne Central)

'How are you all coping?' she settled for instead.

'Getting there—slowly.' Luke shrugged. 'It's good to be back in Melbourne, having my family here and everything.'

'And how are the twins?'

'Getting there, too,' Luke gave another tight shrug, 'though, very slowly. Anyway, enough about me—how are you doing, Molly *Hampton*? Belated congratulations, by the way.'

'Extremely belated…' Molly took a deep breath, always horribly awkward at this bit, and she was almost saved from saying it as around the same time she spoke his eyes dragged down to her name badge. 'It's actually Molly Jones again.'

'Ouch.' He gave a tiny wince. 'Since when?'

'Since a couple of weeks ago. We broke up last year, but the divorce just came through. I figured the time was right to change my name back.'

'I'm sorry to hear that. Any kids?'

'None.'

'Well, that's good.' Luke smiled, unwittingly turning the knife.

'It is…' Molly fished for her mask, that smiling mask she wore quite often. 'It makes things a lot less complicated.'

Only it didn't.

The fact that there were no children was the reason she was minus a wedding ring.

Not that he needed to know.

Not that he'd understand.

'Well, I'm very sorry,' Luke concluded, because he'd gone to private school, because somehow he always remembered his manners, 'for all that you've been through.'

'Let's both stop saying sorry, huh?' Molly suggested, and Luke smiled again.

Smiled because it was Molly.

Smiled because somehow, in a matter of seconds, she'd waved the barriers away.

'So how are you—really?' Luke probed, moving past the niceties and getting to the point.

'Getting there,' Molly answered, then her smile widened, 'Well, I've read every self-help book in the library and I just did a quiz in a magazine and apparently I'm "a woman in control" so I'd say I *am* just about there! So what are you doing now—registrar, consultant…?'

'Heavens, no.' Luke shook his head. 'There's

a registrar position coming up here that I've applied for—I'm just filling in to cover annual leave as a resident for now—and they've lumbered me with a month of nights.' He must have seen her frown. Five years ago it would have made sense—five years ago Luke had been coming to the end of his paediatric rotation; five years ago he would have been starting to apply for a registrar's position—but now? It didn't make sense, and Luke filled in the silence with an explanation. 'With the twins and everything, I had a crazy idea of being a GP—well, that was the plan. I started doing some shifts at a local walk-in, walk-out clinic to see if I'd like it and, well, the money and the hours were good.'

Since when had Luke cared about the money or the hours? Luke Williams had lived and breathed paediatrics—would have done it for nothing in Molly's opinion. Not that he wanted her opinion, she reminded herself—not that he wanted her. Luke had made that stunningly clear five years ago.

Five years almost to the day, in fact.

When he'd walked into the café and after a few choice words had walked out of her life.

Walked out on *them* as he'd run back to Amanda.

'Are you ready to check the IVs, Molly?' her colleague Anne Marie called out. 'Rita wants to start handover.'

'Coming.'

'So you're doing a stint of nights, too?' Luke asked as they both headed down to the cots area.

'I do permanent nights now. There was an ACN position and I decided to give it a go.'

'You're an associate charge nurse?' She could hear the surprise in his voice and didn't blame him—the Molly Jones of five years ago couldn't have cared less about promotions and the like, and Saturday nights had been for dancing! 'You've done well—you really are a woman in control!'

'Thanks. Well, it's good to see you,' Molly said. 'I'd better go—I want to check all the IVs before handover. No doubt I'll see you soon.'

'No doubt.'

Molly always checked the IVs before handover, hated them bleeping and going off during it—hated the day staff leaving and then finding out there was a query with an order or rate and having to ring them at home. And it made handover a lot easier if she had at least glimpsed the patients. It was just something she did and usually very quickly—only not tonight.

Tonight the IV round took for ever, Molly having to check and recheck everything, reeling, just reeling, at having seen Luke again. She'd wondered how she'd feel if she saw him again. When she'd heard that he'd moved back, Molly had wondered if, after all these years, after all that had happened, he'd have any effect on her—had convinced herself almost that the intense feelings she'd had for him all those years ago had been nothing more than a crush.

Some crush!

Her mind whirred back to that dangerous place. When life had been just about perfect.

When for three months, three glorious and

passion-filled months, she'd held him—and been held by him.

Had lain in his arms and been kissed.

Had kissed him back without reservation—safe in the knowledge, that this wonderful, breathtaking man was as into her as she was into him.

Had given every little piece of herself, because she'd *known* he was worth it.

'Did you not sleep today?' Anne Marie's Scottish accent was, Molly was sure, as broad as it had been the on the day she'd landed in Australia twenty years ago!

'I had a great sleep.'

'She's miles away!' Anne Marie winked at Bernadette, a twelve-year-old who'd been on the children's ward for three weeks now with osteomyelitis—a particularly nasty bone disease, which in this case affected Bernadette's femur. Despite rigorous treatment that had required not just IV antibiotics but surgical intervention too, it was a long slow process to get her better, and the young girl was going to be on the ward for quite a while yet. 'Molly's off in a dream world of her own,' Anne Marie carried on, but not even Anne Marie's good-natured jesting could raise a smile from Bernadette tonight.

Still, her mind wasn't on Luke or anything other than work when they came to cot four. Rita, the charge nurse for the day, was exchanging a frown with Molly that didn't bode well, while talking reassuringly to the baby's mother. 'I'm going to ask Dr Williams to come and have another look at Declan. Amy…' Rita turned to one of the day staff '…could you stay with Declan while I give handover? Give us a call if you're concerned.'

'I'm not happy with that little one,' Rita continued once she'd spoken to Luke and they were in handover. 'He's going to be taking up a lot of your night. Declan Edwards, eight weeks, born at thirty-six weeks gestation so a touch prem, was admitted at lunchtime with bronchiolitis and he was doing well till a little while ago—IV fluids, oxygen, minimal handling—but his O2 sats have started to drop. I called Tom, the resident, and he had another look at him an hour or so ago and we increased the oxygen rate, but he's still struggling. I'm glad Luke's just come on, actually…'

Handover on a children's ward was always long and detailed, with not just the children but their families to discuss and endless reams of tiny information that might be relevant at two in the morning when a two-year-old was crying out for his purple bear or, as in tonight's case, a normally happy twelve-year-old whose mood had suddenly changed.

'Bernadette's been pretty low this evening,' Rita said as they came to their last patient at handover, 'which is to be expected, given the length of time she's been here, but she was fine right up until lunchtime. She's had lots of visitors, though. She might just be having a quiet night.'

'No, I noticed she seemed pretty flat when I checked the drips,' Molly agreed.

'All the children in her bay have been discharged so maybe she's feeling a bit lonely. I've told her that we'll soon fill up, and Mum spoke to her before she went home, but she says she's OK, just tired. I don't want to nag her. Everyone's entitled to an off day!'

'It's just not like her, though, is it?' Anne Marie said. 'She's such a bubbly, happy wee thing.'

'We'll keep an eye on her.' Molly didn't bother to write it down, neither did Anne Marie. Both knew their patient well enough not to need reminding.

'Well, I hope you have a good night,' Rita said, handing over the keys to Molly, 'though I think Declan's going to keep you busy. Still, it's good that Luke's on—I can't believe he's just a resident! You remember Luke…' Rita trailed off, obviously having just remembered that Molly would remember Luke Williams rather well. But even though she didn't elaborate, that was all it took for Anne Marie to pounce the second Molly had allocated the staff and was pulling the drug trolley out.

'So!'

'So, what?' Molly blushed.

'That dishy doctor you were talking to before handover—why would *you* remember him?'

'Because he used to work here.' Molly shrugged. 'Before your time.'

'Before Richard's time?' Anne Marie asked perceptively, barring Molly's access to the door. 'When you were young free and single, perhaps?'

'Perhaps!' Molly said tightly, pushing forward, deciding that if Anne Marie didn't move, she'd just run her over with the drug trolley, but Anne Marie stood back, smirking as Molly bulldozed past. 'Hey, Molly.' Anne Marie tapped her shoulder. 'You still are!'

'Are what?' Molly frowned. 'Am what?'

'Young, free and single.'

'Wrong…' Molly gave wry smile, strangely close to tears all of a sudden. 'I'm older, wiser and very newly divorced. Believe me, Luke Williams is absolutely the *last* thing I need right now!'

Though it *was* good to have him on duty tonight.

Good, because a poor excuse for a boyfriend he might have once been but he was an excellent doctor.

Young Declan had Molly suitably on edge and even though Anne Marie was looking after him, the drug trolley was quickly locked and put away, when Anne Marie called Molly over to say that even during handover his condition had deteriorated. His rapid respiration and heart-rate, combined with nasal flaring, indicating he was struggling, despite the oxygen tent he was in.

'Where's his mum?' Luke asked as Molly came in with a head box which would deliver a higher concentration of oxygen to the infant as Anne Marie spoke on the phone.

'She's in the parents' room, ringing Declan's dad. I told her to have a coffee and that you'd come and talk to her soon.'

'Where the hell's Doug?' Luke whistled through his teeth as he urged his consultant to suddenly appear. 'I rang him half an hour ago—he should be here by now.'

'Do you want me to page the anaesthetist?'

'I've paged him.' Anne Marie gave a tight smile. 'Twice. He's stuck down in Emergency and we're waiting for the second one to finish up in theatre.'

And whoever thought night shift was about sitting at the desk and guzzling chocolate had never done it.

Had never worked night after night with skeleton staff and patients that were just as sick at night as during the day, only without the resources to match it. With Molly and Anne Marie tied up with Declan, the ward was being watched by Louanna, a division two nurse, and Debbie the Grad. Most of the senior medical staff had long since gone home and the ones that were here at the hospital were clearly tied up elsewhere.

There was a thin line between a sick baby and a really sick one, and as Luke picked up one floppy, mottled leg, Molly knew Declan was crossing it.

'Ring ICU,' Luke said.

'There isn't a cot,' Molly said, because she'd already checked. 'There will be in an hour or so.'

'Get them on the phone for me.'

Which she did.

And Luke explained in no uncertain terms to a unit that was being run ragged that unless they cleared a space soon, they'd be running to answer a crash call.

'Making enemies, Luke?' Doug Evans, wearing shorts and T-shirt and hauled away from wherever he'd been, looked nothing like the paediatric consultant he was. He was an extremely nice doctor and a very diligent one, too, and everyone, except Declan, breathed a bit more easily as soon as he arrived.

He examined the little babe gently as Luke gave his boss the background.

'I just want some blood gases and then we'd better get him over to ICU. Thanks…' he glanced over to Luke '…for calling me in.'

'Always happy to see you, Doug!' Luke gave

a tight smile. 'Molly, can you come and talk to the mum with me?'

And the dad!

Having raced along the corridor, Mr Edwards burst into the ward, his eyes shocked when he saw his son, especially as at that moment Doug happened to be sticking in a needle to do a quick set of blood gases.

'What's that? What's going on?'

'That's called a head box,' Luke said calmly. 'It's to give your son a higher concentration of oxygen and we're just taking some blood gases. I'm Dr Williams. I was just about to talk to your wife, if you'd like to come down to the—'

'I'm staying here!' Mr Edwards barked. 'You can tell me what's going on here.'

'No, I can't,' Luke answered easily. 'Declan needs rest and to be kept quiet and I don't want any tension around him.'

'I'm fine! I just want to know what's going on.'

'Well, come down to the parents' room and I'll tell you, along with your wife.' And without further word he turned and walked out, politely, calmly, but making it absolutely clear he wasn't going to change his mind. And after a very short time, Mr Edwards followed.

'Wow!' Anne Marie gawked in admiration. 'I'm going to *like* working with Luke Williams. Off you go!'

'Press the bell if you need me.'

'Sure.'

Lucy Edwards was very different in nature from her husband—a calm woman, she actually seemed relieved when Luke explained that their son was going to be transferred to the intensive care unit.

'But he was fine when I left.' Mr Edwards looked appalled. 'I want to know what the hell happened.'

'He just suddenly got worse, Mike.'

'Why?' Mike said accusingly. 'You're supposed to get better in hospital.'

'And he will,' Luke said firmly. 'But bronchiolitis, especially in such a small baby, often gets worse before it gets better—and your son needs more monitoring and support than we can adequately give him down here on the ward. He needs one-on-one nursing, and if he does deteriorate further I'd far rather he was already in Intensive Care, with doctors and an anaesthetist to hand, than have us putting out an emergency call at two in the morning.'

'But he'll be OK…?'

'With the right treatment and the right care,' Luke said calmly, 'which is what he'll get in Intensive Care, where he should do well.'

'He will be OK?' It was Lucy asking now, tears and fear starting to catch up with her, and though no one could guarantee anything, Luke's quiet assurance was what was needed. 'He just seems so tiny…'

'He's struggling right now,' Luke agreed, 'and the next twenty-four to forty-eight hours are going to be difficult, but I fully expect him back on the ward with us in a couple of days. The best thing we can do now is get him moved up there, get him settled.'

He made it all so straightforward—he always had, Molly realised as within half an hour she had resumed the drug round as a little entourage trooped to ICU with their precious cargo. Utterly confident in his own decisions, and utterly willing to admit when he couldn't work miracles, he'd never been one to waste time calling in help or transferring a sick child.

But that was Luke, Molly thought with a mental sigh as she added some antibiotics to Bernadette's flask and upped the rate—decisive, straight to the point.

And when he decided he didn't want you any more, he wasted no time in getting to the point, no time beating around the bush—just scheduled a transfer and breezed out of your life.

'How are you feeling?' Molly smiled down at the girl, noticing her red eyes and pinched face. 'Not too good, huh?'

'I'm just...' Bernadette gave a frustrated shrug '...fed up.'

'I don't blame you.'

'Stupid leg….' Bernadette sniffed. 'It's never going to get better.'

'It will,' Molly said. 'It's just taking a long time.'

'What's idio—idiom—?'

'Idiopathic?' Molly said, and Bernadette nodded. 'I heard the doctor saying it to my mum. What does it mean? Have I got cancer?'

'No, you don't,' Molly said firmly, wishing that grown-ups would think about little ears before they bandied big words about. 'It's nothing to be scared of. Idiopathic means "no known cause". Osteomyelitis can be caused by injury or trauma, or by an infection that spreads—only in your case they haven't been able to pinpoint any reason or find out why it happened.'

'And that's all that it means?' Bernadette checked.

'That's it.' Molly nodded.

'Well, I hate idiopathic…' Bernadette kicked her good leg in frustration and Molly knew exactly what she meant.

Knew because she hated the word too.

Hated it that there was no reason the doctors could find that she couldn't have babies—hated it that there was nothing wrong, which meant there was nothing that could be fixed.

'Is there anything else worrying you, Bernadette?'

'No.' Bernadette took a breath and for a second Molly thought she was about to tell her whatever else it was that was troubling her, but Bernadette changed her mind and shook her head. 'It doesn't matter.'

'It does to me.'

'You wouldn't understand.' Bernadette turned her face away, crossed her arms over her chest and promptly set off the IV alarm. 'I don't want to talk about it.'

'You're getting all tangled,' Molly said, straightening out the tubes and resetting the IVAC. 'We've got a new patient coming in—a six-year-old with a head injury. I've put her next to you.' Normally Bernadette would have a million and one questions—what had happened, what was her name, did Molly need her to look out for the new patient, to press the bell? Only not tonight. Tonight Bernadette just shrugged one tight shoulder and carried on staring at the wall.

'Even if I might not understand,' Molly said to the back of Bernadette's head, 'if you decide that you do want to talk about it, press the bell.'

'Talking's not going to help.' Bernadette sniffed. 'It doesn't change things.'

'I don't agree. Sometimes talking to your friends can change things.'

'You're just a nurse, though.'

'I'm your friend while you're here,' Molly offered. 'If you want me to be. Mind you, I should warn you that I'm not very good at sharing, and I'm not really in with the in crowd…' Pleased to see a near smile on Bernadette's pale lips, Molly chose not to push it. 'Up to you.'

'So you used to work here?' Anne Marie had made coffee, opened a packet of chocolate biscuits and was interrogating Luke by the time Molly finished her round and sat down. 'How long ago?'

'Five years.' Luke didn't look up from the notes he was writing, but he did take a biscuit or three. 'Then I moved to Sydney.'

'Why?'

'My wife's family lives there.'

'Oh!' Deflated, Anne Marie looked as if she was about to snatch back the biscuit he was holding as Molly gave frantic eye signals to tell her to stop. 'So you're married?'

'Widowed.'

'Oh!' It was a very different 'oh' this time as she pushed the whole biscuit packet in his direction. 'Do you have children?'

'Twins!' Luke said abruptly. 'Angus and Amelia—they're four.'

'How?' Anne Marie asked, as only Anne Marie could. 'What happened?'

'She was run over.' His lips were tight, his face grim as he wrote, but Molly knew that if he hadn't wanted to answer then he wouldn't have, knew that he was probably grateful in some way for Anne Marie's rather oddball directness, that he probably just wanted to get it over with. 'It happened six months ago. She was a doctor here too.' He looked up from the notes and to Anne Marie, 'You might remember her. Amanda Metcalfe.'

'Anne Marie's only been here a couple of years,' Molly said quickly.

'I arrived just in time for all this madam's dramas!'

'Dramas?' Grateful for the change of subject, Luke actually smiled. 'Oh, your divorce.'

'It's nothing to grin about!' Molly scolded, but she was smiling too.

'What a sad lot we are…' Anne Marie dunked her biscuit in her coffee.

'You too, then?' Luke asked, because—well, Anne Marie was waiting for him to! 'What's your tale of woe?'

'I haven't got one.' Anne Marie pouted, standing up as a patient bell went. 'Dead boring, me!'

'I don't think so somehow.' Luke grinned as she wandered off. 'Is she always that direct?'

'Always.'

'Well, at least it saves me from telling everyone. I'm sure Anne Marie will take care of that for me.'

'She won't—believe it or not, she's actually really discreet. She is,' Molly insisted as he gave a rather disbelieving frown. 'So, how does it feel to be back?'

'Weird!' Luke said. 'Familiar but different. Hard to explain, I guess.'

He'd done a very good job. It was so, so familiar, sitting at the nurses' station, gossiping, smiling. It unsettled Molly how easily they'd slipped back into ways of old, chatting easily, sort of friends again, yet it was so, so different.

Sipping her coffee, every now and then she looked over to where he was working, his blond hair falling forward as he wrote his notes.

Five years ago she'd loved him.

Absolutely, with all her heart loved him.

Had longed to get to work in the morning just to see him.

Had held her breath when she'd heard he'd broken up with the gorgeous Amanda.

Had almost fainted when he'd asked her out.

Had then longed to finish work just to be alone with him.

'Hey, I was just thinking…' He looked up, with green eyes that had once adored her, and Molly burnt the roof of her mouth taking too big a gulp of her coffee. 'Do you want to get breakfast after work in the canteen? We've got a bit of catching up to do.'

There was no right answer, Molly realised as she replaced her mug on the bench. If she said no, then he'd know how much he'd hurt her, might guess that as of three hours ago she'd realised that she wasn't actually over him. But if she said yes—well, sitting across the table from him, just the two of them, he was probably going to work it out anyway!

'I can't,' Molly settled for instead, grateful that

she actually had an excuse. 'I'm meeting Richard for breakfast tomorrow.'

'Richard?'

'My ex,' Molly explained.

'That's very civil.'

'We are,' Molly said, squealing inwardly in delight at how well she'd handled that one. OK, she wasn't thin and in her cocktail dress, but *somehow*, for the first time in her entire life, she'd managed to play it cool!

'Another time, then,' Luke said.

'Sure.' Brimming with new-found confidence, she even managed a smile as she casually stood up and slowly walked off, only letting out her breath and breaking into a burning blush when she finally made it the restroom.

Contained—the elusive word she'd been looking for to describe Luke popped into her head.

He looked more contained than the laughing, care-free doctor she'd fallen head over heels in love with.

Tireder, sadder, older…a little more contained.

And why wouldn't he be, given all that had happened? Molly thought, staring into the mirror at her own reflection. With a jolt she recognised that the sparkle that had been absent for so long was back in her eyes, her heart was fluttering that little dance that it hadn't for the longest time, and she had a slight smile on her full mouth and that lovely, euphoric feeling that came when you either drank champagne or…

Oh, no!

She really didn't have time for this.

Didn't have time to be flirting and blushing and wondering where, how, or if it was going anywhere. And she really, really wasn't ready for this.

CHAPTER TWO

'OFF for your breakfast?' He was walking along the corridor beside her.

'I've got to drop the car at the mechanic first for its service. Yes, then breakfast. What about you?'

'Race home, get the twins dressed and then take them to kindergarten, then bed.'

'So what are they like?' Molly asked because she was interested. 'The twins.'

'Different as chalk and cheese.' Luke grinned. 'Angus is practical, serious. Oh, he has fun and everything, but he's just straight down the line…'

'And Amelia?'

'Dramatic!' Luke rolled his eyes. 'A right little minx, actually. She's got me completely wrapped around her little finger—and she knows it.'

'Sounds like fun.'

'Not lately.'

And they stopped.

Stopped in a corridor, and for the first time really looked at each other.

'I'm sorry.'

'We're not saying that—remember?'

'Even so.' She couldn't look at him now and scuffed the floor with one of her feet. 'I know it's hard sometimes, hard pretending that you're OK…'

'It is,' Luke agreed.

'*Telling* everyone that you're OK,' Molly ventured.

'Just because they want to hear it,' Luke finished.

And even if they weren't, as they started walking Molly felt as if they were holding hands.

Holding hands through turbulent times.

Not that she'd been alone.

Friends had rallied round and family had gathered when Richard had walked out, walking out on them. On her.

There had been life rafts aplenty as she'd drifted for a while.

And, yes, they'd steered her to a place that was calmer— a place that was safe, where she'd hidden for a while—only now came the hard bit.

And only the lost could understand.

Trying to survive on an island that was empty.

Trying to keep warm with a fire that kept going out.

And trying to fathom if you could ever risk the journey again.

'I miss the casseroles.' Luke nudged her into a smile as they walked on. 'The mums at kinder set up this roster.'

'I miss the cakes.' Molly smiled. 'And the take-aways. I don't think I cooked for a month!'

'So do you two do that often, then?' They were stepping out into the ambulance bay, blinking as if they'd just come out of the movies at the bright morning sun—both talking fast, both on that slightly euphoric high that came at the end of a night shift when you should be tired, but you're not. 'Richard and you, do you meet up often?'

'No…' Molly thought about it for a moment. 'Just when we've got something to discuss, but that's getting less and less often now.'

'It's good that you can still be friends.'

'Oh, I wouldn't call it that.' Molly grimaced. 'To tell you the truth, I'm not looking forward to it all.'

'Text him, then,' Luke half joked and half dared. 'Give him some lame excuse and come and have breakfast with me instead.'

'Why would I even bother to text him?' Molly joked back, but she was walking to her car. 'Surely if there's one person you can stand up without guilt or lame excuses, it's your ex.'

'Well?'

They were at her car and she was surprisingly tempted to do just that. Funny…a night of gentle flirting with Luke and she'd forgotten to be nervous about meeting Richard, but she was wanting to get there now, wondering what that he wanted to discuss and sort of knowing what it was too.

Torn between convincing herself she was just being paranoid and bracing herself to face up to the truth.

'I'd better go.' There was more than a hint of regret in her voice. Luke this morning was an infinitely preferable option to hearing whatever it was Richard wanted to *discuss*. Luke's green eyes were tired but smiling, and he needed a good shave, and he looked like he'd looked in the mornings. Apart from the clothes and the packed car park, she could almost imagine his face on the pillow beside her.

'Ooh, is that the time?' Molly pretended to look at her watch. 'I'd better get a move on.'

'You know, it's actually nice, being back.' Luke smiled down at her. 'And it's been really nice to see you. I wasn't sure how you'd be, after what happened and everything.'

'It was a long time ago,' Molly pointed out, 'and given all that's happened to you, well…'

'I don't need your sympathy, Molly.' He said tightly. 'It's just good that we seem friends again—which we were. I mean, we were good friends…before.'

Before.

One little word that didn't quite match the passion and the pain it stood for—but it was far safer and far easier to relegate it to that. Far easier to just call it *before* than to actually discuss it.

'It's good to have you back,' Molly agreed. 'And you're right—it's good that we're friends.'

'Thanks for coming.'

'No problem!' Molly lied, slipping into the chair opposite Richard. 'It's good to see you.'

There were a million and one self-help books and Molly had surely read them all, but not one of them could actually do it for you.

Not one of them could actually tell you how to walk into a café and face your ex, whether you should kiss him on the cheek, or not, shake hands, or…just do as Molly did and pick up the menu and pretend to read it.

Not one of them could actually be there for you when, despite appearances, despite the bright smile, despite the brave face, Molly knew this was going to be another of the blackest days of her life.

'There was something you wanted to tell me?' Ordering her latte, Molly scanned the menu, trying to decide whether to get honey on muffins, or the cinnamon toast, perhaps, which was always nice.

'It's a bit awkward.' Richard took a deep breath as Molly read on.

'I might get the scrambled eggs. Ooh, or maybe mushrooms on toast.'

'You see, I didn't want you to hear from anyone else. I thought it was right that I be the one to tell you—'

'I might just go the whole hog and get—the full breakfast, please.' She beamed at the waitress. She'd sworn she'd be cool for this moment, had prayed, had pleaded to any god that might be listening that she'd somehow manage a smile and congratulations when she heard that Jessica was pregnant, but she couldn't do it, couldn't sit there and smile, so instead she cried, just promptly burst into loud tears as Richard peeled off napkins and handed them to her. It made her feel worse, not better, that he was blowing his nose too, that his eyes were glassy and he was taking her hands and holding them.

'I'm so sorry, Molly.'

'Don't say that!' she sobbed. 'Because you shouldn't be sorry, you should be happy. This is good news. It's good news!' she said again, because it was. Richard had always wanted to be a dad, would make a wonderful father. He shouldn't have to be apologising for something wonderful.

'I know.'

'And I'll be fine.'

'I know. I just know how much this must hurt.'

'You don't know,' Molly said, because he didn't any more. He'd joined the ranks of parents-to-be, just as, it seemed, everyone did in the end—everyone that was, but her. He'd seen her when she'd managed to smile at her sister's happy news, had held her hand when she'd visited friends in hospital, and had held her after, when she'd sobbed her heart out. Had held her and told her that one day, *one day*, they'd get there, be the parents they wanted so badly to be.

Well, now he had.

'I'm happy for you!' She managed a very watery smile. 'I know I don't look it, I know I'm probably embarrassing you…'

'You could never embarrass me.'

'But I really am very happy for you,' Molly gulped. 'You deserve this.'

And he did deserve it.

But, then, so did she.

The marriage hadn't ended because she hadn't been able to have a baby—over and over she'd told that to herself. Richard wasn't some bastard—as so many had made out—who had left her because she couldn't give him babies. They just hadn't been strong enough to survive the struggle, the endless, endless tests, the tears, the letdowns, the depression, the hell that was infertility.

He was a nice guy and she was a nice girl and they just hadn't made it.

'I'm actually not that hungry.'

'Don't go, Molly.' He was still holding her hand as she stood to go. 'I know—'

'No, Richard, you don't.' Molly shook her head and pulled back her hand. 'Please, don't make me sit here and reassure you that I'm OK. I will be OK. I just need to get through this bit—and I want to do it on my own.' And she turned to go, but changed her mind, turned around just in time to see a flash of relief on his face that this uncomfortable duty was over.

And for the first time she was angry.

Not that little bubble of anger that flitted in every now and then and was quickly quashed. Instead, this big pool of bile seemed to be being stirred up inside her, and she waited for a second, tried to swallow it down, but it just kept rising.

She tried to reason with herself that by the time she walked back across the café to him it would have gone, that she would have calmed. She could see the nervous dart in his eyes as she marched back towards him and actually asked the question that had been churning for weeks in her mind.

'Is that why you filed for divorce?' She sat back down as Richard jumped to attention. 'I mean, you didn't waste a moment, did you? A year to the day exactly, the second you legally could, you filed the papers—you did. Are you getting married?'

'Jessica wants us to be married before the baby comes,' came Richard's logical answer. 'It's important to her.'

'But not very important to you.' She wasn't crying now, was sitting like a headmistress peering down her nose at a rather wayward child as the waitress brought her breakfast. 'Clearly, Richard, marriage isn't very important to you.' And if she hadn't embarrassed him before with her tears, she was doing a *much* better job now.

A dull blush spread over his cheeks as her voice got louder and a couple of heads in the crowded café turned and looked. 'We can all *say* the right thing, we can all stand at the altar and *say* for better, for worse, in sickness and in health, we can all console ourselves that we're doing the right thing, and that we're being terribly civil and understanding by comforting our poor infertile ex-wife when the new tart's pregnant—but you know what? It's not about what we say, Richard, it's about what we *do*!'

'Then I tipped the whole lot, beans and everything, in his lap…' Molly sobbed on her mobile five minutes later to Anne Marie.

'Good for you!'

'And then I told him he could bloody well pay for breakfast!'

'Good for you.'

'I got really angry, Anne Marie. I mean really, *really* angry.'

'About time.'

Shutting the curtains on the bright morning sun, Molly bypassed the self-help books and turned off the phone. She grabbed a box of tissues, then climbed into bed. As her cat climbed up for a cuddle, Molly shrugged him off, then climbed out of bed and put him out of the room.

She didn't want to be some old spinster who kept cats, didn't want to feel so hollow and barren and less of a woman than she'd ever felt in her life

She *was* over Richard—despite having said it so many times. Like a big spear being pulled out of her side, Molly knew now that she finally was.

It wasn't Richard—it was her babies she was crying for this morning.

CHAPTER THREE

'MAYBE you could use a friend?' Bernadette was way too knowing for such tender years and at two a.m., when Molly was giving her her IV, two eyes had peeped open and said what no one else had dared. With Anne Marie on a night off, not one of the staff had commented on her very swollen, very puffy, heavily made-up eyes, and no one had mentioned Molly's impressive red nose and swollen lips—even Luke, apart from a small frown when he'd seen her, had had the decency to ignore them, but kids weren't so subtle.

'I'll be OK.' Molly smiled.

'I probably wouldn't understand anyway but, as you said, sometimes it's nice to have a friend.' Bernadette's eyes filled with tears, and Molly realised, with a sinking heart, that she finally wanted to talk, which was good and everything, just terribly bad timing.

'What's going on, honey?' Molly said.

'You won't laugh?'

'Not tonight,' Molly assured her.

'You'll probably say I'm too young…'

'I won't. Is it a boy?'

'I thought he liked me. And then Carly came and said that they're going out, that they're going to the movies in a group, but she said that he's told her that he likes her—and she knew I liked him…'

'What's his name?'

'Marcus. I just hate being here, and I hate feeling like this.'

'Have you told your mum?'

'I told her I liked him ages ago, before I got sick, but she laughed and said I was too young for all that sort of thing. That I didn't *really* like him…'

'But you do,' Molly said simply.

'And I don't know what to do.'

'Cry?' Molly suggested, but really kindly, sitting on the bed and holding Bernadette's hand. 'Eat a lot of chocolate…that's what I do.'

'Does it help?'

'No!' Molly shook her head. 'Well, sort of—in the end you do feel better, but I don't know if that's the crying and chocolate or if you'd have felt better anyway.'

'I really do like him. I know I'm only twelve—'

'Hey, I fell in *love* at eleven!' Molly countered, and if she'd not been giving Bernadette her full attention she might have heard Luke come in to the room, might have seen two shoes appear beneath the curtains, would have caught his eye as he poked his head around and told him without words that unless it was urgent she'd be there in a few minutes. But instead she carried on talking. 'His name was Darren and he was gorgeous. He had big hazel eyes with really long eyelashes and sort of slightly buck teeth, but they suited him. Anyway, my friend Leslie said he was awful. He asked me if I was coming ice-skating on the weekend and I said I had to check with my mum. Well, I had to go to a christening and on the Monday I found out that Leslie had gone ice-skating and the next thing I knew…'

'Were you really upset?'

'I cried for a month,' Molly said. 'In fact, I could cry right now, this very minute, when I think about it. He was lovely. He still is.'

'You know him now?'

'Vaguely.' Molly shrugged. 'He's married to Leslie and they have a farm, so it worked out well, really—I don't think I'd be a very good farmer's wife.'

'Why?'

'I'd forget to set the alarm clock in the morning or something—and the cows wouldn't get milked and would probably end up with mastitis. I'm not very good with animals.'

'So it was probably for the best.'

'Probably.' Molly nodded. 'Only it didn't seem that way at the time.'

'So you really have felt like this! But it gets better, doesn't it?'

'Duh!' Molly pointed to her swollen eyes. 'Hey, Bernadette, strap on your seat belt because you're in for a bumpy, horrible ride, but it's fun too and exciting at times—wonderful, in fact.'

'It doesn't feel wonderful.'

'It will.' Molly smiled. 'And then it will be awful again for a while and you'll swear off men for life, then the next thing you know…' She gave a little shrug. 'I'm probably saying all the wrong things and scaring the life out of you.'

'It's nice to talk, though,' Bernadette sniffed. 'I actually do feel a bit better!'

'Friends do that for you,' Molly said, and stood up. 'Cry, eat chocolate and talk to your friends—but choose them carefully.'

'Carefully?' Bernadette frowned.

'You'll work it out.'

'Oh, you mean…'

'The Carlys and Leslies of the world!' Molly

nodded. 'I'd better go. I've got a baby to feed. I'll talk to you later.'

Oscar Phillips was one of those gorgeous chunky babies who just lived to be fed, grabbing at his bottle with two fat hands, his mouth and eyes wide open before Molly had even sat down at the nurses' station.

'Don't worry, Oscar, food's coming,' Molly assured the baby, glad when Luke came past and picked up the phone, which was ringing.

'Hello, Mrs Phillips. He's being fed at this moment!' Luke grinned down the phone. 'He seems fine. I'll just check with the nurse who's looking after him.

'It's Oscar's mum, just checking in,' Luke mouthed to Molly.

'He's been good.' Molly nodded as Luke relayed the message and chatted with Oscar's mother for a moment or two.

'Thanks for that.' Molly sent a weary smile to Luke.

'Anything else I can do for you?'

'Nope.' Molly shook her head. 'You might even get some sleep.'

'No chance. I've got a couple of kids down in Emergency that need admitting and I want to go and check in on Declan over on ICU.'

'How's he doing?'

'Better,' Luke replied. 'I think they might send him back to the ward tomorrow. I'll pop up later.' He turned to go, then changed his mind. 'And, by the way, I think you'd have made a lovely farmer's wife.'

'Luke!' She was genuinely appalled. 'Were you listening? That was private!'

'I couldn't help myself.' He laughed. 'I came to see if you had anything else for me to do—then I heard you talking and realised I probably shouldn't disturb you. And then…' He stopped laughing and looked at her, and she could feel his eyes taking in every bit of make-up and somehow taking in with it every bit of her brave face. 'I think you'd be a wonderful farmer's wife and even if you're not very good with animals, you're wonderful with children. You did a great job in there.'

'Poor little thing.' Molly smiled in the vague direction of Bernadette's room.

'And what you said was right,' Luke said gently. 'It really is good to talk to friends.'

'I know,' Molly said. She knew what he was offering only she couldn't take it. 'But not just yet.'

'How about breakfast?'

'I really *don't* want to talk about it.'

'Then don't,' Luke said. 'We can sit in silence if you want. I'll meet you in the canteen after your shift. No excuses.' His pager shrilled, making little Oscar's eyes, which were starting to close, pop open. Luke gave a wry smile as he pulled it out of his pocket. 'Except this one!'

Declan behaved, Emergency behaved, even Luke's pager behaved, which meant that twenty three hours, practically to the minute, since she'd had breakfast with Richard, Molly sat with a coffee, in a room full of people, with a man she'd once loved, and tried, once again to be brave.

'I'm not going to talk about it.' She stabbed at the plate of bacon, eggs, sausages and mushrooms he'd plonked in front of her.

'Fine,' Luke said, attacking his own breakfast. 'There's no brown sauce.'

'There never is. Here…' Molly pulled a few sachets out of her apron pocket. 'I nicked some from the ward. Actually, if you knew what happened yesterday, you might have thought twice about buying me a cooked breakfast.'

He didn't say anything, was busy buttering his toast and then ladling the entire contents of his plate, beans and all, into a vast sandwich, which was what he'd always done, Molly remembered. Unlike her, who left her toast to the very end and used it to mop her plate.

'I threw the lot in his lap.' She watched him smile with a very full mouth. 'You probably think I'm awful now.'

Luke swallowed. 'Did he deserve it?' he asked.

'I'm not sure—but I thought he did at the time.'

'Then I don't think you're awful.' He stared at

her plate, and her hands, and there was just a tiny flicker of nervousness in his eyes. 'Eat up, Molly.' He grinned. 'There's a good girl.'

'Oh, you don't have to worry! Not that you didn't deserve a greasy lapful at the time, but I'm over you now.'

'Good.'

She gave him a slightly wicked smile. 'And, lucky for you, I'm starving.'

'Well, that's a relief.'

'And we're friends now,' Molly said.

'We are,' Luke confirmed. 'And that's good too.'

'Jessica's pregnant.'

'Jessica?' Luke said carefully.

'Richard's girlfriend. And I'm happy for him, I really am. I mean, I don't even want children, which was the problem in the first place. He wanted babies and I wanted my career.' If she said it enough, one day she'd actually believe it. Anne Marie had told Molly she was mad, of course, that she should lean on more people, let everyone know what she'd been through, was still going through. Only Molly couldn't—couldn't stand the sympathetic looks, preferred people to think it was by choice that she was childless.

'I never realised you were so career-minded!' Luke voiced his surprise. 'You were a great nurse, of course. I just always thought that…'

'What?'

'It just seems a strange choice of career—I mean, to work with children if you don't actually like them.'

'I do like children.' Molly gave a tight smile. 'And then I like being able to come home. Anyway, it doesn't make sense. I mean, if I worked on the oncology ward, it doesn't mean I want cancer.' It was a line she'd used more than a few times, and after a moment's thought Luke gave an accepting shrug and a nod.

'Good point.'

'It was just a bit of a shock, I suppose…' she gave another tight smile '…that he was having a baby. Anyway, it doesn't matter. I'm fine with it now. I'd really rather not talk about it.' She barely paused for breath. 'You see, I think I was so surprised because I thought Jessica was his transition girl.'

'Transition girl? I'm not with you.' Luke frowned, smothering his smile with a forkful of bacon as Molly had just refused to talk about it!

'You know—it's in all the books: after you come out of a relationship, you have your transition person—someone who's just there to help you get over what's happened, to massage your ego, sort of an evolution thing, to help you move on. You both know it's not going anywhere, it's not supposed to be *the one*. And I just assumed that that was what Jessica was.'

'His transition girl?' Luke frowned.

'Yep. Only it turns out she wasn't. They're getting married. Sorry.' Molly was embarrassed all of a sudden. 'I know I go on sometimes.'

'It's good to talk.'

'It is,' Molly agreed, then took a deep breath, forced herself to look at him as she forgot about herself. 'Do you?'

There was a horrible silence, a wave of pain surging towards her as his face creased and he visibly struggled to speak. When he did, he said two words she'd never heard from him.

'I can't.'

Because Luke always *could*, always had a solution to everything—even if meant calling in the boss. There was nothing Luke couldn't do. Except this. Molly felt tears fill her eyes again, only they were for him. Her hands held his and she didn't care if anyone was watching or looking because this wasn't about them, it was about him.

'I can hardly stand to think about it, let alone talk about it.' His eyes screwed closed as he held it all in. 'I just keep on keeping on, for the kids.'

'If you ever do,' Molly offered, 'want to talk about it…'

'I know.' Luke nodded, taking back his hands, even managing a half-smile. He was a little embarrassed, Molly guessed, that she'd glimpsed his pain, and quickly changed the subject. 'So, er, have you had your transition guy?'

'Heavens, no.' Molly mopped up the last of the egg on her empty plate with her toast. 'It's way too soon. Have you?'

'Oooh, there's a question!' He scratched at his chin for rather a long moment and the conversation that had flowed so easily just, *just* tipped into inappropriate—and perhaps that line of topic wasn't the most sensible one to follow, Molly realised, as they both rather awkwardly stood to go and then walked along the corridors and out into the ambulance bay. They stood horribly uncomfortably, facing each other. Perhaps it hadn't been the most sensible conversation to have with your ex.

Who you still really fancied.

Especially when you were a bit woozy from a day of crying and a long, long night shift.

'Where are you parked?'

'At the mechanic's!' Molly answered. 'It took me so long to get to sleep that by the time I woke up…'

'Do you want a lift?'

'I'll get the tram,' Molly said firmly.

'It's really no problem.'

'Don't you have to get home for the twins?'

'They've got kindergarten today—Mum stayed over last night and she's taking them.' He'd pulled out his car keys, was sort of jangling them between his fingers, and if they were just friends, she should just say yes, Molly thought, jump in the car and yawn her head off all the way home. Only they couldn't be just friends, Molly realised, because her heart was hammering in a way it didn't when Anne Marie offered her a lift, and eye contact was suddenly a terrible problem.

'I'll get the tram!' Molly said again, only this time to her shoes, telling herself she was being stupid, that there was no tension between them. Gosh, his wife had just died. As if he was even thinking…

'Molly…' His fingers lifted her chin, his delicious mouth a breath away as he said her name, and then it was on hers, and it felt so right, because it always had, so blissful, so familiar it actually hurt—hurt to taste again what she'd once devoured. She felt a sting of tears in her eyes as she kissed him back—a long slow kiss that neither wanted to end because then there would be questions that neither were really ready to answer. But end it did, and she still couldn't look at him, so she didn't, just buried her face in his chest as he held her for a moment.

'The staff car park's probably not the best place.' She tried a little joke, only it didn't work. 'I have to go.'

'I know.'

And she did have to go—had to walk away that very second without looking at him, had to put as much space as possible between them, before they both went and did something really stupid.

Really stupid, Luke said to himself as he started the car up and swiped his ID at the barrier. He could see her marching ahead, was tempted, so tempted, to wind down his window just to talk to her again. Feeling like a kerb-crawler as he did just that.

'You couldn't afford me.' Molly grinned, a little bit pink, her eyes a bit glassy, but she was smiling again, able to look him in the eye again, able to make him laugh as somehow she set the tone.

'Probably not.' Luke smiled back, and then his face became serious. He knew that a little kiss was big sometimes—that it was probably her first kiss since Richard—and he didn't want to hurt her a fraction more than he already had. 'I actually wasn't about to whistle you in—I was just…' He didn't know how to voice it but, because it was Molly, he didn't really have to. 'You're OK?'

'I will be,' she answered, and because it was Molly she checked on him too. 'You?'

'Same!'

She probably thought he was feeling guilty, Luke realised as he drove off, glancing in the rearview mirror at the woman who consumed him. No doubt Molly thought six months was too soon to be over Amanda. He dragged his eyes back to the road, his face hardening as he indicated right and headed for home.

And for the hundredth, no, the thousandth, or perhaps even the millionth time, in the five years since he'd left her, Luke thought it again.

If only Molly knew.

CHAPTER FOUR

'TO OVERSLEEP once and leave your car at the mechanic's may be regarded as misfortune,' Anne Marie said loudly as they walked into work, and Molly could have hugged her as she fabulously misquoted, because it gave her a very good reason to be blushing as Luke looked up, 'but to oversleep twice can only be regarded as sheer laziness!'

'You overslept *again*?' Luke grinned.

'OK, OK,' Molly grumbled. 'I was exhausted. I just fell straight asleep and forgot to set my alarm.'

'Don't push it!' Anne Marie nudged her as they headed to the locker room. Because of course she hadn't fallen straight asleep—had spent the morning frantically reading her so-called 'help' books then angrily over-plucking her eyebrows while telling herself in the mirror that Luke was an utter bastard and she'd be completely mad to even *think* about getting involved with him again. And what a nerve he had to even think he *could* kiss her. How *could* she have let him?

'Don't leave me on my own with him.' Molly pulled on her stethoscope.

'Why—are you scared of him?' Anne Marie winked.

'Don't be stupid.'

'Scared you won't be able to keep your hands off him, more like! Don't worry, hen, I'll look after you! Anyway, we might be quiet—you might not even see him.'

'I wish.'

You really should be *very* careful what you wish for, Molly reflected as she gave handover the next morning, after an entire night without so much of a glimpse of Luke. Out of twenty-two sick kids not even one of them had managed a raised temperature, not one lousy IV chart or prescription to write up and the two empty beds that, despite a full to bursting emergency department, had remained empty. Even on the two occasions he'd rung to check if he was needed, Debbie or Anne Marie had answered the phone.

How was she supposed to play it cool, Molly huffed, when he wasn't around?

'Rita wants to do my appraisal while the ward's quiet.' Anne Marie rolled her eyes as Molly came out of handover. 'Do you want to go to the canteen and grab a coffee?'

'I'll just get the tram.' Molly yawned, pulling out her hair-tie. 'And I'll remember to set my alarm this time.'

Actually, she'd key a reminder into her mobile, Molly decided, blinking as she stepped out into the bright morning sun, tapping away.

'Oy, have you been avoiding me?' Luke made her jump as he caught up with her and made her smile too. 'What a night! It was steaming in Emergency.'

'I wish we'd been busy.' Molly yawned again,

because now she'd started she couldn't stop. 'You know, I'm more tired when I'm doing nothing.'

'Stop it!' Luke scolded, also yawning. 'Now look what you've done.' He gave her a very nice smile, but Molly couldn't help but notice he didn't offer her a lift. 'See you, then.'

'See you.' Molly smiled.

'Sleep well!'

'I will.' Molly nodded, wishing her legs would move and wishing his would too, but still they stood there. 'You sleep well too.'

'I will.'

'Right—see you then.' She was really going this time—well, she would have, Molly decided if he hadn't *then*, very casually offered her a lift.

'Sure.' Molly shrugged. 'But only if it's not out of your way.'

'Not at all.' Luke also shrugged. Only it was—miles and miles out of his way, as it turned out, because of course even if she hadn't completely moved on in other ways, she'd moved house several times since they'd last been together.

'Left here…' Molly sneaked a surreptitious look as she gave directions. She didn't usually like blond men, only he was so tall and so big and so…just so Luke. Actually, he could have come in orange with green stripes and he'd still have made her toes curl. 'And then a quick right at the roundabout.'

His mind clearly wasn't on the road, because he missed the quick right and they had to go round the roundabout again—Molly rigid and leaning back, trying not to lean into him, moving her hands quickly when he moved his to change gear, even frowning at the dashboard, because according to that he had climate control on…only she was roasting.

Maybe his climate control wasn't working, Molly thought helplessly as her house loomed into view. Well, obviously it wasn't working, because Luke was turning up the fan at that very moment, blasting them both with a shock of cold air that surely hissed into steam the second it hit their cheeks.

'Here!' Molly croaked. 'I'm the house before the white car.'

'Right!' Luke nodded, missing it by a mile and having to execute a hasty U-turn. 'Is this the one?'

'That's the one.' Molly beamed, scrabbling in her bags for her keys. 'Thanks ever so much for the lift.'

'My pleasure.' Which made him sound like he was giving a political speech! 'So you live here?'

'I do!' Molly's smile was rigid. 'Er, do you fancy a quick one?' Her face went from red to purple as Luke gave her a rather startled look. 'A quick coffee or something—before you drive home, I mean.'

And he lost a zillion brownie points at that point. The million-dollar lottery dropped to a few cents as he faltered with indecision.

They'd driven fifteen kilometres, for goodness' sake. *Surely* he should have worked out his answer to the inevitable question before they got there. *Surely* he should be the one dealing with this—should have smiled and said no, or should have already turned off the engine before they headed inside.

‘Whatever.’ Molly beamed to his rigid profile. ‘I guess I’ll see you at work tonight…’

She never got to finish, never even got her keys out of her bag. A wedge of muscle was suddenly pinning her against the car seat, a mouth was knocking the breath out of her. Had there been any breath, Molly thought faintly as his tongue reacquainted itself with hers—because she’d stopped breathing at the roundabout. But, God, it felt good, he felt good, they felt good. The lottery payout ding-a-ding-dinged as it rose—a sort of battle with arms and legs and confined space, and neighbours putting their bins out and a dog barking.

‘Coffee?’ Molly croaked again, pulling back as she completely gave in.

‘Sounds marvellous!’

Keys really were the most ridiculous, unevolved things. It was the twenty-first century, for goodness’ sake, Molly thought as she smiled and waved at her neighbour and tried to get the sliver of metal into the smallest of slots—tried to stop the cat as he shot for freedom, tried to just make it through the front door.

'Coffee?' She turned as they entered, said it yet again, with conviction. There was for a while a sliver of hope that they might make it to the kettle—but Luke didn't even deign to answer. Just grabbed her and kissed her all the way to the bedroom.

And what a mess it was!

Littered with self-help books, a magnifying mirror and tweezers on her bedside table and—of all the *awful* things to have on display—her bed was awash with tissues, tiny sodden balls that screamed of pain. But he dusted them away with one hand, cleared the mattress in almost one stroke, before an angry cat almost took his hand off.

'Hell!' Luke cursed, sucking on the scratch as for the second time in a couple of days the cat was deposited out of the bedroom, but for such a nice reason this time.

'I'm supposed to be playing it cool,' Molly whimpered as he grabbed her again.

'You're not cool, though,' Luke breathed. 'You never were,' he added between kisses. 'Don't ever change.'

And whoever said you shouldn't go back to your past was wrong, Molly decided as she frantically stripped off his clothes and he did the same to her. Whoever said that sex for sex's sake ultimately didn't satisfy had never had a six-foot-three Luke Williams raring to go in their line of vision. Whoever said that ultimately she'd regret it might just well be right, Molly accepted as he kissed away her pain, as his tongue slid over her body and washed away the years—but she'd deal with that later. And, yes, her bottom and boobs were just a little bit bigger than when last they'd met, but Luke didn't seem to mind a jot.

'Oh, Molly, I missed you!'

He wasn't supposed to say that, Molly thought helplessly. This wasn't supposed to be about looking back or looking forward. This was supposed to be all about now.

'I missed you too,' Molly admitted, even if she shouldn't.

Oh, but she had.

Missed his sexy body, missed how he made her laugh, missed, missed, *missed* that he could be so into her, ravishing her, tasting her, grabbing handfuls of flesh as if he needed it to survive.

'I want you so much…' He just groaned it out. They were kneeling on the bed, grabbing at each other, kissing each other, revelling in each other. And then he just gathered her towards him, and the theory was it was way too quick and way too soon, but it was exactly how she was feeling.

'I want you too,' she whimpered, just holding him in her hand, guiding him into her, leaning on him, wrapping herself around him, lost in her own feelings but utterly safe and sound, awash with her own orgasm but drowning in his, feeling him within her and somehow knowing that what was happening was big.

Very big.

And very scary, because according to Luke she was still hung up on Richard, and according to Molly he was still grieving for Amanda.

Her head was on his chest, his blond chest hair on her cheeks, his arm holding her, and she could only guess at the expression on his face. She could feel the pensiveness in the moment, and wondered not just what he was thinking but who he was thinking about. But she was too scared to look and not ready to ask.

'Don't ignore me at work tonight.' Wriggling out of his embrace, she turned on her side, stared up at her bedside table, tried and failed to fathom that Luke was here in bed beside her.

'Why would I ignore you?' He was making tiny circles with his fingers in the small of her back.

She ignored his question and carried on speaking. 'Because you might regret it.'

'Not for a second.'

'I might,' Molly said.

'Ignore me or regret it?'

'Both…' She was playing with one of her curls, pulling it out to its full length then letting it ping back, thinking out loud and trying hard to be honest. 'I just don't want to get involved.'

'Er, at the risk of stating the obvious—' Luke started.

'I mean,' Molly broke in, absolutely aware they were lying in bed, absolutely aware they had just had sex and no doubt they would again, but possibly more scared than she'd ever been in her life. Because losing Luke, losing Richard, *that* she could deal with, *that* she had dealt with, only staring over at him, staring into those jade eyes, feeling him all big and strong and male beside her, feeling the peace his body brought hers, it was her mind she was scared for, because giving herself back to him, only to lose him again, would be too much to bear. 'What I'm trying to say is that I don't want to get involved like we were…' She swallowed hard, could hardly bring herself to go there in her mind, let alone say it. 'Before.'

'Molly, I know I hurt you. I know—'

'Don't.' She brushed his hand away. She could take affection, could take intimacy, even—she just wasn't ready for tender, lust-filled explanations. Just couldn't, wouldn't go there with him.

Because she already had.

She had given him her heart once and he hadn't treated it kindly, hadn't handled it with care, and she wasn't going to take that chance again.

CHAPTER FIVE

'HEY! Fancy seeing you here?' Luke had a point—midday in the admin corridor was the last place Molly would usually be. 'And looking very smart too!' He ran an approving eye over her chocolate-brown suit, and Molly shifted in her nipping high heels as he took in her bare, fake-tanned legs then dragged them back up to her for once carefully made-up eyes—slightly awkward eyes that couldn't meet his.

He'd rung her a couple of times since that morning, had tried to talk to her at work, but Molly either hadn't picked up or had been too busy.

And it wasn't about playing it cool this time—it was about playing it safe.

'I had an interview,' Molly mumbled. 'What about you?'

'Same.' Luke indicated his own very nice suit, 'Well, a first one anyway.'

'How did it go?'

'You never really know, do you? I can expect to hear from them shortly! How about you?'

'Same.' She could actually look at him now.

'So what was the interview for?'

'It's for a paediatric intensive care course—there are quite a few applicants, and most of them already work in Intensive Care, so I'm not that hopeful.'

'How long's the course?'

'A year—a pretty full-on year too. Still, it's something I really want to do—need to do,' Molly corrected herself, 'if I want to get on.'

'You are getting on.' Luke smiled. 'Fancy lunch?'

'No kids?'

'Mum's taking them to her sister's after kinder so I've got a couple of hours. Come on, we'll take my car and I'll drop you back here afterwards.'

Which was nice and easy.

So nice and easy that when they were sitting

in a pub in their smart suits, tucking into steak sandwiches, Molly even managed to relax.

'We look like business people!'

'We do!' Luke grinned. And it was just something they did—or used to, Molly realised, people-watching or playing stupid little role-play games that didn't need the rules set out—because somehow they already knew them. 'Having a lunchtime meeting! What are we discussing?'

'My fantastic performance!' Molly winced at the opening she'd unwittingly given him.

'It was!' Luke winked. 'And the figure's certainly pleasing, and you're definitely easy to get along with…' He took a long drink. 'But…'

'There's always a but.' Molly sighed.

'I'm a bit concerned about your inability to commit—and communication hasn't been effective lately.'

'Ah-h, that!' He'd always been able to do that, Molly remembered, always been able to get straight to the point and soften it somehow. Maybe there was a reason they liked their silly games, because it made those difficult things just a touch easier to say. 'Well, I'm not looking for anything permanent at the moment.'

'Molly.' He wasn't playing any more. He put down his drink and took her hands as she spoke to their fingers.

'I was very happy with the company,' Molly said, playing but not playing too. 'But not at the way my role was terminated. So…'

'I'm sorry for hurting you. Things were so, so-o…' He took one hand back, rubbed and then squeezed the bridge of his nose with his fingers, as if holding it in as he forced the words out. 'It wouldn't be like that again.'

'Because there's no Amanda to leave me for.' And there wasn't much he could say to that, so he didn't.

'So what happens now?'

'You drop me off, then pick up the twins, and I'll go and grab some sleep before work.'

'That wasn't what I was asking.'

'I know.' Molly gulped.

'Do you want to see me again?'

'Of course I do.' Molly's answer was so assured Luke was confused.

'But you said you didn't want to get involved.'

'I don't,' Molly said, and it took half a glass of lemonade before she was ready to explain further. 'I guess we just accept that we're not going to go anywhere. You know what we were talking about before—maybe we could be each other's transition person…'

'Oh, please,' Luke groaned.

'Why not? We've both been through a lot. A no-strings affair where we both just enjoy each other for as long as we….' she blew her fringe skywards '…enjoy each other, I guess.'

'Massage each other's egos?' Luke checked, and she nodded. 'Make each other feel good?'

'Sounds about right,' Molly said. 'And of course there'd be lots of fabulous sex!'

'Friends as well?'

'Absolutely.'

And in theory it sounded perfect, only Luke

was gritting his teeth and sort of shaking his head. 'I don't know if I can do that. I mean, I don't know if that's enough for me. I really like you.'

'You were right before—you *really* did hurt me, Luke.' There, she'd said it, and because she'd said it once, it made it easier to say it again. 'You really hurt me—and I just don't know if I can get past that. I don't know that I could ever really trust you again—if I even want to try to trust you again. And then there's…' Her voice petered out and he took over.

'The twins?' he said, and she nodded. 'And that's not you?'

'It's not.'

'Could it ever be?'

'No,' Molly said honestly, because even if she wanted a baby, even if she wanted children, even if she'd met him for the first time today and he'd come with his own mini-football team, she could have accepted them. But they hadn't met today. They'd met five years ago—and she didn't want to raise Amanda's children.

Didn't want to raise the children of the woman he'd walked out on her for.

Didn't want to suddenly be good enough now that Amanda had gone.

And those were the rules—or her rules, at least—and for a little while he thought about it, his expression closed and unreadable until he leant across the table.

'Come here, transition girl.' He gave her a kiss, a very nice, very slow kiss that almost made her feel better—especially when he pulled back, especially when he looked into her eyes so deeply it burnt. 'We'll stay friends… whatever happens.'

'Of course we will.'

CHAPTER SIX

THREE short bursts on the patient buzzer had Molly locking the drug trolley and running.

'He's convulsing.' Louanna had pulled down the cot-side on the bed and had Bodey on his side, was turning on the oxygen at the wall as the little boy jerked and grunted. 'I was walking past and heard him.'

'He's burning.' Molly felt the hot little head as she held the oxygen mask over his rigid face. 'Fast-page Dr Williams!' Molly said as Anne Marie, alerted by the buzzer, ran in and grabbed the resus trolley. 'Louanna.' But she was already onto it, pulling the curtains around the other patients' beds so they couldn't see what was taking place. But though the four-bed ward was unusually empty, Molly caught a glimpse of Bernadette's pinched, worried face as again she was witness to just a bit too much.

Molly gave little Bodey rectal diazepam, which he had been written up for in an emergency. Debbie cool-sponged him, while the little body jerked beneath them. 'Where's Mum?'

The question was answered by Bodey's mother's arrival, a moan of fear escaping her as she dropped her sponge bag.

'He's having another seizure,' Molly said calmly, as Debbie went over to her. 'He's going to be OK. He's got a temperature.'

A convulsion was a fairly routine emergency. Some babies and children were prone to them when they were febrile. But no matter how used the nurses were to dealing with them, they were still unpleasant and just awful for the mothers, and Debbie led Bodey's mother out to the corridor just as Luke arrived, breathless from running from Emergency.

'How long—?'

'Five minutes since we found him,' Molly answered, glancing up at the wall clock. 'He's had some rectal diazepam. I gave him some paracetamol five minutes before that.' The fitting was stopping now, the awful grunting and rigidness abating. Bodey dragged in big deep breaths and his rolled-back eyes started to shut. 'Bodey Andrews, five years old, admitted with a febrile convulsion following a query UTI,' Molly said. As night cover, it wasn't possible for Luke to know every patient and their history off the top of his head.

'Right…' Luke checked Bodey carefully, looking in his eyes, ears, his throat…flicking through the blood work that had been done in Emergency. 'Well, there's an infection somewhere. Have we got anything back on his urine yet?'

'I'll check on the computer, but nothing's come to the ward yet,' Molly said.

'What's he been like overnight?'

'He's slept. Afebrile at two, just woke up grizzly at half past five, so I gave him paracetamol.'

Bodey was starting to wake up now, scared and crying as Luke continued to examine him, pushing his head down onto his chest. 'Let's get some blood cultures now, while he's febrile.' Luke frowned in concern. 'Let's get him down to the treatment room—can you pull up his path results for me? And send his mum down. I'll talk to her there.'

'Is he okay?' Bernadette asked, once Bodey had been moved to the treatment room.

'He will be,' Molly said, 'though it must have been horrible for you to see.'

'I could hear him making all these noises, but I was asleep. I thought he was just snoring. Maybe I should have pressed the bell…'

'It's not your job to watch the patients!' Molly said firmly. 'And he did sound like he was snoring. These things just happen with little ones sometimes, when they get too hot. He's going to be OK.'

Only Luke wasn't so sure.

'He doesn't like the way he's holding his head,

so he's going to do a lumbar puncture.' Anne Marie, now in a gown and mask, stuck her head around the door. 'And he's called Doug to come in.' Anne Marie's face was serious. 'You know we've had two with meningitis in the space of a week—remember the little one you specialled?'

How could she forget?

She had been called on her day off to see if she could do some overtime—specialling meant one-on-one nursing. In this case it had been for a child with a stent infection who had a complicated history of cerebral palsy and seizures—a child who had, it turned out, after Molly had spent a frantic night in a closed room with him, actually had bacterial meningitis and due to Molly's close contact with him she had had to be treated with antibiotic cover. 'I'm still on antibiotics.' Molly grimaced. 'But it happens like that sometimes. We don't even know if that's what's wrong yet!'

'I know,' Anne Marie sighed. 'Just my brain working overtime.'

It was just one of those really horrible mornings where nothing got done, and worse, Molly chewed over whether she had done enough for Bodey. He had been grizzly and febrile when he'd woken up, but had settled back to sleep, so much so that his mum had nipped out for a shower. And the dipstick on his urine had indicated a urinary tract infection, which would account for his temperature. All of this whirred through Molly's head as she gave out the drugs and ran errands for Anne Marie when she popped her head out of the treatment room more than a few times.

'We're moving him over to ICU.' It was Doug who stuck his head out this time. 'Could you ring and let them know we're leaving now?'

Which didn't go down too well. ICU had only just heard about the patient, but when Molly explained the consultant himself was bringing him over, there wasn't much they could say.

'Remind me again why I'm applying for a permanent job here?' Luke's face was grim as an hour later he raced back to catch up on his notes.

'How is he?'

'Seized again just as we got him over,' Luke said. 'Doug's with him now and so is the anaesthetist. I've got to write up some notes and hand over to Tom.'

'Emergency rang. They're sending up a patient in half an hour,' Louanna called out. 'Nathan Tomkins is thirteen years old. Where do you want him?'

'I told them not to send him till the day shift got here.' Molly ran an exasperated hand though her hair. They'd had two admissions from emergency at five a.m., then Bodey had had his convulsion and taken a bad turn, and with the day case theatre patients starting to arrive it had thrown the morning routine out of the window. And now this. 'I'll ring and tell them that they're going to have to wait. We're just too busy. And he's for traction, so the bed's going to take for ever to set up…'

Unfortunately, Molly never got to the phone. Emergency's version of half an hour differed from that of the rest of the world by about twenty-nine minutes. The ward doors opened and the new patient arrived, whether the children's ward was ready or not.

And it would serve no purpose getting angry in front of the patient, so Molly greeted Nathan warmly and told him they wouldn't be long, then, silently fuming, went to the storeroom, where Anne Marie was trying to scramble together the traction equipment.

'Thanks!' Molly let out an angry breath, then helped her colleague haul down the massive metal frame that would sit over Nathan's bed and the bracket that would support the weights. 'Imagine sending him at a quarter to seven in the morning.'

'ICU said exactly the same thing,' Anne Marie pointed out. 'But that's Emergency for you!' Anne Marie rolled her eyes. 'You know how busy they are, unlike the rest of the hospital.'

'Where shall we put him?' They were carrying the equipment between them, trying to come to rapid decisions that usually merited a bit more thought.

'In with the boys in room eight. Or he could go with Bernadette—she's sick of seeing people come and go, poor wee thing,' Anne Marie tutted. 'I was talking to Luke. He just got some blood back on her and he said that she's probably here for *another* fortnight at the very least. She could probably do with someone who's here for a while, but she's got her period, and I'm sure the last thing she wants is to share her room with a boy.' It was a juggling act that went on all the time in the children's ward—trying to balance teenagers with toddlers, boys with girls, long-stay patients with overnighters, and sometimes it was impossible, but they did try to get the mix as close to right as they could. Molly whizzed down to talk to Bernadette before she made her choice.

'I just thought it might be nice for you both to have some company around your own age—given that you're both going to be stuck here for a while. But if it's awkward for you with bedpans and all that…'

'No, no.' Bernadette was already sitting up in bed, waving to her new roommate through the glass window. Nathan was giving a sort of half-wave back. 'Bring him in.'

'You get on,' Anne Marie said to Molly, grinning at Bernadette's cheerful expression. 'Louanna and I will set up the traction and get him settled.'

Molly never really caught up after that. After giving handover, even though she was aching for bed, there were more than a few patient notes that needed to be updated before she could get there.

'Morning, Molly!' Tom, the resident, all nice and refreshed from a night in bed, grinned as he surveyed the chaos. 'You look exhausted.'

'Tell me about it!' Molly said, not even looking up from the notes she was writing.

'Actually, Luke, I was hoping to ask a favour…' Luke gave a grunt that sort of matched with Molly's mood as Tom went on. 'Any chance of you swapping so you work Saturday night for me? It's our wedding anniversary and I completely forgot and Shelly will never forgive me if I'm working—you know what it's like.' He halted suddenly. 'Sorry, Luke, I just didn't think.'

'It's fine.' Molly looked over as Luke gave a tight smile and managed a brief shrug. 'And it's fine about Saturday too. Actually, if you could do a weeknight for me, that would be great. Just makes things easier.'

Only it wasn't fine—in fact, it must hurt like hell, Molly realised, because not only was he juggling work and raising twins and doing everything that Amanda must have done, he was grieving for her too.

'Does it hurt all the time?' They were lying in bed, half awake and half asleep, and Molly could almost hear Luke's mind whirring.

Could feel the tension that, even after their love-making, hadn't left him this time.

'Not when I'm with you.' His face turned towards hers, jade eyes holding hers.

'Do you think about her all the time?' Molly asked, and watched his eyes become shuttered.

'Molly…' He gave an exasperated sigh. 'Where are we going with this?'

'I'm just trying to understand…'

'Well, you don't.' He sat up in the bed, dragged his hands through his hair. For a second she thought he was going to climb out, but instead he confronted her with a truth. 'You know, for someone who wants to keep things light, you're asking some pretty heavy questions.'

'I know.'

'I just don't want to go there, Molly.' He shook his head as she stared over at him. 'That's about Amanda and I…and it's not something I can share with someone who doesn't want to get too involved.'

This time he did get out of the bed, leaving Molly more confused than she'd ever been because, like it or not, deny it or not, getting involved was exactly what she was doing.

With her heart.

'What are you doing with these?' Luke came out of the bathroom, holding up a packet of antibiotics.

'They're rifampicin…' Molly blinked.

'I know what they are. I just didn't know you were on them.'

'That child who had bacterial meningitis…' Molly's throat was suddenly dry. 'Not Bodey—there was one last week when you were on nights off. I was specialling him before we knew what it was…' Her voice faded out, knowing exactly what he was thinking. She'd let him think she was on the Pill—and if she was on the pill then a week's course of rifampicin meant they should be taking extra precautions.

'And you didn't think to tell me!' Luke snapped. 'Or you just didn't stop and think. For heaven's sake, you're a nurse, Molly.' He was really angry now, pulling on his clothes. 'You want to be more careful, you know, because for someone who doesn't want to get involved, for someone who definitely doesn't want kids, you're walking on very shaky ground.'

* * *

Very shaky, Molly realised when later he rang to apologise, to check that she was OK, being nice and concerned, and just Luke.

'I wasn't the best anyway this morning.'

'Well, it wasn't exactly the best night to work.'

'You're telling me.' She could almost see his eye-roll. 'When I was taking the history his mum said something and it turned out that Bodey's little sister goes to the same kinder as the twins.' Luke sighed into the phone. 'I've just rung Doug and it would seem that Bodey's meningitis is more likely viral—the infection showing up in his blood work is actually from his UTI. But I left there this morning thinking there was a meningitis outbreak, wondering if I should send the twins to kinder today, just completely over-reacting—you know what it's like.' He gave a soft laugh but it was aimed at himself. 'Oh, no, you don't, do you? You probably think I'm crazy.'

'Anne Marie was the same.' Molly's voice was unusually high.

'Kids…' Luke sighed. 'Who'd have them?'

And he hung up the phone with all the confidence and neurosis of someone who did.

Yes, very shaky, Molly realised, swallowing her antibiotic, telling herself that if he knew he wouldn't make such careless remarks, and telling herself that maybe it was time that he did…

CHAPTER SEVEN

'WHAT was she like?'

Doing their bit for the environment *and* their purses, since the mechanic debacle, Anne Marie and Molly had decided to take it in turns now and then to give each other lifts—but they were stuck in traffic, due to a crash on the freeway, and Anne Marie was asking questions as they crawled along at two kilometres an hour. Molly rather wished the emissions coming from her friend were from the exhaust pipe.

She'd been seeing Luke for a couple of weeks now, and because Anne Marie knew everything anyway, Molly had, of course, told her, making her cross her heart and hope to die that not only would she promise not to breathe a word but that she wouldn't interfere—which Anne Marie was extremely good at.

'Amanda—what was she like?'

'I never really got to know her.'

'But she worked with you.'

'Not much. She was from Sydney. She'd come to Melbourne for a paediatric rotation, but she only stayed for six months, and half the time she was on sick leave—there was some family problem in Sydney she had to keep flying back for.'

'Still, you must have formed an opinion.'

'Superwoman!' Molly finally admitted.

'Tell me.' Anne Marie grinned at Molly's tense profile. 'What was Superwoman like?'

'Good-looking, funny…' Molly changed into second gear and the engine let out a groan of protest as they finally moved a couple of hundred metres. 'Thin, tall, blonde.' The car in front's brake lights weren't working, which made things even more difficult, and they jerked forward in their seats as Molly slammed on her brakes and ground the gears, along with her teeth.

'Intelligent, witty, sexy, organised…' Stalling in the middle of the freeway, Molly put on her handbrake and restarted the engine, praying the service on her ancient car had actually achieved something. It had—the car started again and the conversation resumed.

'Basically, she was everything I'm not.'

'So you hated her?' Anne Marie laughed.

'Sadly, no,' Molly sighed, nodding her thanks to the police officer who had waved her onto the hard shoulder and past the accident, 'though not for want of trying. She was also extremely friendly and nice— Oh, do you think we should offer help…?'

But nothing, not even a pile-up on the freeway, was going to stop Anne-Marie. She wound down her window and after a brief chat with the police officer, who said that everything was under control, turned her attention back to the—for Molly—painful subject.

'You were saying?'

'That we're going to be late,' Molly attempted, and Anne Marie didn't push, didn't say anything.

But maybe she *did* need to talk, maybe what had eaten her up for so long now really did need to be voiced.

'Luke and I were friends—really good friends. We just hit it off the day we met. I had a bit of a crush on him, well, any female with a pulse did, but he was already going out with Amanda when we met, and I knew I didn't stand a chance—it was nice to just be friends. Then suddenly they broke up. Out of the blue. I heard that they'd broken up and that she'd gone back to Sydney.'

'And?'

'We had a sick kid in one day—I know we have sick kids all the time but…' Molly's voice thickened for a moment at the memory. 'She died. I know it happens, I know we all deal with it, but we were both pretty upset. The next day was my day off, but that evening the phone rang—he'd got my number from the ward book and he rang to see if I was OK.' Molly frowned. 'We were friends at work, that was all, so ringing me at home was crossing the line. He asked if maybe I wanted to go out for a drink.'

'Which you did?'

'I was more than happy to cross the line.'

'You got on well?'

'Wonderfully well.' Molly sighed. 'We were only together for three months, but for the entire time, from the first date, we were inseparable. We were already friends and that just got better. It wasn't just sex, though that was great, and it wasn't just the romance. I can't really explain it...'

'Sounds a bit like love,' Anne Marie said, and Molly sniffed loudly as she indicated to leave the freeway, because that was exactly how it had felt, at least to her. 'I was worried at first. I mean, I wanted to know that they'd actually split up, that she wasn't just in Sydney and they were taking a break, but, no, he told me they were washed up, that there was absolutely no chance of them getting back together. Then one Friday I was on a half-day and he rang and asked if we could meet. I thought it was strange. I mean we never actually formally *met*, it was either his place or mine, but we met in this café and he told me he'd made a mistake, that he was moving up to Sydney to be with Amanda and that it was over…' And even though she could tell Anne Marie almost everything, that bit she couldn't. Even five years on the words were too painful to repeat to herself, let alone someone else.

'Do you think she was pregnant? Do you think that's why he went back to her?'

'Probably—I don't know the twins' birthday, but I've done the maths and I guess she must have been.' The sign for the hospital blurred. Molly turned in, swiping her ID for the staff car park, and even though they were late as she pulled into her usual spot, neither woman made a move to get out. 'If he'd told me that, I could have understood. If he'd said that he had to make a go of things, I could have taken that.'

'Could you?'

'I think so.' Molly sniffed again. 'I mean, it would have hurt, but I would have respected why he was ending things. But, Anne Marie, what we had was good, so-o-o good. I utterly, utterly fell for him, held nothing back for myself, and never, not for a second, did I see it coming. When he rang me, when I met him that day, it never even entered my head that he was about to end things. And it wasn't just that—it was *how* he ended it. It doesn't matter.'

'I think it does.'

'Not now…' Molly gave a grim smile. 'But if I've learnt anything from it, it's that I'll never trust him again.'

'Which isn't a very good basis for a relationship.'

'We're not in a relationship, though,' Molly pointed out.

'Come off it, Molly. You see each other all the time, you're sleeping together, you're both clearly crazy about each other—if that's not a relationship, then I don't know what is.'

'OK, maybe we are in a relationship of sorts, but I know this much—he'll never have that piece of me again.'

'What piece?' Anne Marie frowned.

'That piece you give of yourself. That piece of yourself that you normally don't let anyone else see, that piece of yourself that you trust the other person to take care of.' There was a wistful note to her voice as she recalled all they had shared, all they had once been, but her lips pursed with a bitter tinge of aftertaste, even after all these years.

'Be careful,' Anne Marie said, and Molly wished that she hadn't, wished Anne Marie would tell her she was being stupid, tell her, as she always usually did, to go for it, that it was time to live, time to get out and have some fun.

'Hey.' Molly tried to make light of it. 'Weren't you just saying the other week that I should get out there, start dating?'

'And move on from the past,' Anne Marie elaborated. 'And, yes, I know Luke's gorgeous, and I know he clearly likes you, it's just…well, he didn't treat you well.'

'I know.'

'And you deserve to be treated well.'

'I know that, too.'

'Just don't settle for anything even close to second best. Look, maybe I'm worrying about nothing.' She relented a touch. 'Maybe, with losing his wife, he's been through enough hell to come out a different man.'

It was scary how much Molly wanted to believe that he had, scary that, despite firm words, somewhere deep inside she was wavering, wanting to give him that piece of her she really ought to hold back—and wanting too that piece of Luke that, until she opened up, he wasn't prepared to give. 'Come on.' She heaved her bag from the car floor and opened the door. 'Or we'll be *really* late.'

'What's all the noise?' Molly asked sternly. 'I told you two to settle down half an hour ago.'

'Sorry!' Bernadette didn't look remotely sorry.

'Sorry…' Nathan mumbled. 'We were watching a movie…' He started laughing again and so too did Bernadette. Molly stood between their beds and looked up. They both had a television over their beds and had taken to wearing their headphones while watching the same show and shouting ever louder at each other.

'What are you two watching?' Molly asked, hoping that, given the lateness of the hour, she hadn't let them get away with watching something completely inappropriate. But it was one of her favourite comedies too, and Molly couldn't help but giggle herself as, even without headphones, she easily got the joke.

'Keep it down,' Molly warned as she left them to it.

'We've got a direct admission coming in.' Luke came into the kitchen to find her, where she was rummaging in the hospital fridge, trying to find some juice and sandwiches for one of her post-op patients who had woken up hungry. 'Carl Adams—an eight-year-old with asthma. That was his GP—he's seen the child several times over the past week and can't get it under control. He's coming in directly from the GP's to the ward.

He's been in a few times.' He must have seen Molly's slight grimace. 'He'll be stuck down there for ever if I send him to A and E. There's been a big pile-up on the freeway and—'

'I know all that,' Molly agreed, 'but I'll be down a nurse for a while, because no doubt you'll want a chest X-ray.'

'No doubt!' Luke made no apology.

'I think I recognise the name,' Molly said. 'He was in a few weeks ago, actually. I'll ring Admissions and have his notes sent up.'

'I want a drink.' The spotty, moody face of Aaron Bowden peered round the door and made her jump.

'Please!' Luke stared over at his patient, who shouldn't be in the staff kitchen anyway.

'Please,' Aaron mumbled, taking the can of lemonade Molly offered. With Luke still staring, he offered a quick 'Thanks.' Then added, 'Oh, and my television isn't working.'

'I'll ring Maintenance in the morning.'

'But I was in the middle of watching a film!'

'It's eleven o'clock—you should be in bed,'

Molly said, but Aaron just blinked at her and she gave in with a sigh. 'They're watching it in Room 2. Go and get your headphones. I'm sure they won't mind if you join them, but I'm telling you, and you can tell them, that if I have to come in about the noise again, all televisions are going off.'

'Thanks,' Aaron mumbled, without prompting this time. 'By the way…' His face was as red as his pimples as he turned to Luke. 'How was that kid—the one who had the fit the other morning?'

'Doing well.' Luke smiled. 'He should be back on the ward tomorrow.'

'Still big on manners, I see!' Molly grinned when Aaron had gone.

'Absolutely!' Luke nodded. 'Aaron's a nice kid under all that hair—he just comes across badly.'

'He's a teenager!'

'A teenager who's getting himself into all sorts of trouble,' Luke pointed out. 'I spoke to him last night. You know, I think he's really bright.'

'Aaron?' Molly frowned, wondering if they

were talking about the same patient. 'He's failing in everything at school…'

'Because he's bored out of his skull, probably. I was taking some blood from him earlier and the news was on—they were talking about interest rate rises or something. I was only half listening, and he came out with a really smart comment. I nearly missed his vein. It was something really observant that you wouldn't expect a fifteen-year-old to say.' His eyes widened, along with Molly's. 'Especially Aaron. I'm going to see about getting him evaluated. I'll have to speak to his mum first *and*…' Luke grinned '…if I have unearthed a child genius, he's going to need a few manners when he goes for a scholarship interview.'

How could he have just given it all away? For the hundredth, maybe the thousandth time she asked herself. For some quick money? For convenient hours? Had he gone on to do the GP rotation she could have understood—his own patients, following them through, getting to know their families. All of that, Luke would have adored, but a walk-in, walk-out clinic just wasn't him. A script for antibiotics and a sick certificate for work for a nameless face wasn't the way Luke practised medicine.

Aaron Bowden was in for burns to his hands and neck—thanks to a stupid home experiment in the garden while he'd flunked school and his mother had been at work. The usual! But Luke had taken time with the young man. Had sat and chatted to him one night when a children's ward was the last place a teenager wanted to be, when it seemed every baby in the place was awake and all the toddlers were crying for their mums.

Luke had sat in the playroom with him.

Had turned down the chance for a precious couple of hours of sleep to play video games with Aaron and get to know him.

That was the sort of doctor Luke was—the sort of man he was.

And he was also a man who could reduce her to jelly with just a few choice words…

'Right…' He drained his glass. 'I just need to sign a chart for Anne Marie. Call me when the new admission gets here.'

'Please!' Molly called to his departing back, but he ignored her. 'Please!' she said more loudly, which, as Luke turned round, she realised had been his intention. Her breath caught in her throat when he turned round and gave her *that* look—*that* look that told her and only her exactly what he was thinking—and topped it off with a tiny, knowing wink.

'Save the begging for later, Molly!' He grinned at her blush as he twisted her words deliciously. 'We're at work, remember?'

'What are you looking so flustered about?' Anne Marie asked when Molly came back to the nurses' station where a completely relaxed Luke was signing off the drug charts.

'I'm just hot,' Molly said, pointedly taking off her cardigan, then frowning when Luke came back onto the ward. 'And keep an eye on Room 2—there's a party going on.'

'They could use one!' Anne Marie said. 'And so could you!'

'Sorry?' Molly frowned.

'When was the last time you went to a party?' Anne Marie dunked her biscuit in her coffee as Molly pursed her lips. She knew what Anne Marie was up to, but she'd promised not to interfere, and she would have reminded her of that fact except Luke was standing there—Luke, who didn't actually know that Anne Marie knew. 'When was the last time you had a fabulous night out somewhere really nice?' Thankfully a call bell went and Anne Marie, as if butter wouldn't melt in her mouth, stood up. 'I'll get it.'

'That told me.' Luke gave a half-smile to her departing back. 'She's right.'

'She's meddling,' Molly said, 'which is what she does best. Is everything OK?'

'Everything's fine. I was just wondering…' He nodded his head towards the playroom '…if I could have a quick word.'

'Sure.' They never brought their relationship to

work. Obviously Anne Marie knew, but apart from a quick flirt when they were alone, their *relationship* was strictly off the ward. Still, as Molly duly headed for the playroom, somehow she knew this wasn't about work.

'My mum's got an appointment at Outpatients this morning—at eight. It's at the Women's Hospital.'

'Is she OK?'

'She's having a few tests—nothing too serious, I think.' He gave a low laugh. 'And I'm not being evasive. It doesn't matter to her that I'm a doctor. As she keeps telling me, there are certain things she refuses to discuss with her son—whatever his profession.'

'Good for her.' Molly smiled, but there was a worried tinge to it. 'Are you concerned?'

'A bit,' Luke admitted. 'Still, if she doesn't want to talk to me about it, I'm not going to push it—for now, at least. She's going to be dashing to appointments for the next couple of weeks so I'm just letting you know that I might be a bit pushed.'

'Of course.' Molly gave a confused frown. 'You don't have to worry about upsetting me. I'm not that needy!'

'You're not needy at all.' He gave a wry smile, a look she couldn't quite interpret flicking over his features, but it faded before Molly could even attempt to read it. 'The thing is, I've cleared it with Rita, and Mum's going to drop the twins off at seven. I finish at eight, so they're *hopefully* going to amuse themselves in the playroom for an hour till I get off.'

'Great.' Molly beamed, but she could feel her heartbeat quickening, nervous somehow at the prospect of meeting Luke's children and desperately trying not to let it show. The children couldn't come into this, and it was important she keep things light, treat the fact he was bringing his children into work just as she would if it were any one of her colleagues. 'So what's the problem?'

'Problem?' Luke checked.

'You said you'd already cleared it with Rita.'

'I have.' Luke nodded. 'I just thought I should let you know—that you might feel a bit…' He gave a quick shake of his head. 'It doesn't matter.' As she turned to go he called her back. 'This weekend—you're off?'

'So are you.' Molly grinned, but it faded when she saw his expression.

'I don't think I'm going to be able to see you, Molly. I could maybe ask Mum if she can have the twins on Saturday night, only I seem to be asking her an awful lot, and I haven't really seen enough of the twins, with doing nights.'

'No problem.' Molly's smile snapped back on.

'But it's your birthday on Saturday.'

'How do you know…?' Molly frowned, because she deliberately hadn't told him. Deliberately, because birthdays and flowers and intimate dinners and celebrating milestones weren't what they were about.

'Some things you just remember. Look, I will try and arrange something.'

'There's really no need,' Molly said firmly.

'I've been neglecting my friends a bit of late. You enjoy the weekend with the kids.'

'Well, if you change your mind…' There was just a hint of emotion on his usually deadpan face. 'I mean, if you fancy kicking a ball around the park with the kids…then we could get a take-away or something…'

And it would be so, so easy to say yes—she was desperate for her days off and was really looking forward to catching up with her friends on Friday and hitting the shops, yet despite the smile, and despite the fact she'd played it down, it did matter that it was her birthday. It meant that this massive aching abyss wouldn't be filled till Monday. She wanted to see him, didn't want to wait till their shift ended on Tuesday morning, or till the kids were safely at kinder on Monday and he could knock at her door. Oh, she wanted him, wanted him in her bed, wanted to be in his, but she wanted more than that too.

It was Luke who broke the endless silence. Luke who drew the wrong conclusion when she didn't instantly respond. Luke who inadvertently saved her from herself. 'Am I right in thinking that footy's not really your thing?'

'These are the only flat shoes I own.' Molly clicked together her sensible navy nursing shoes. 'And I'm catching up with—'

'It's fine,' Luke interrupted. 'You don't need to explain your movements to me.'

Only she wanted to.

Wanted to be more important in his life as much as she wanted him to have a bigger place in hers.

Still, there wasn't time to dwell on it. By the time the ward was settled for the night Carl had arrived. Molly could hear him wheezing from the other end of the corridor as the paramedics wheeled him in.

'Young Carl.' The paramedic smiled as Molly approached. 'You're expecting him?'

'We are.' Molly smiled a welcome, but one glance at her new patient and she was reaching for the phone in her pocket. Carl was beyond being anxious, he was too exhausted with concentrating on his breathing to even notice his surroundings. Leaning forward on the stretcher, he was using his accessory muscles to breathe, and his eyes were closed, his whole body clearly drained from the exertion. This was one sick little boy, and the treatment room was the best place for him—all the equipment was to hand, and on a children's ward any procedures tended to be undertaken there so as to minimise distress to the other children, especially at night when hopefully the ward was sleeping.

'He's gone downhill in the ambulance…' The paramedic met Molly's eyes and she gave a brief nod. 'Let's pop him into the treatment room. Hello, Mrs Adams, I'm Molly, the nurse in charge tonight.'

'Where's the doctor?' Mrs Adams didn't return the greeting. 'I thought you were expecting us?'

"We are,' Molly responded. 'Dr Williams is over in Intensive Care at the moment. I'll let him know that you're here.'

'But he knew that we were coming.'

Two hours ago, Molly wanted to point out, tempted to tell Mrs Adams that her son wasn't the only patient under Luke's care but knowing that the woman's rather brusque manner was probably masking her anxiety.

'Anything I can help with?' Anne Marie's face was welcome as she came into the treatment room.

'Could you settle Carl and take the handover from the paramedics?' Molly answered with just a hint of raised eyebrows as the phone trilled in her hand. 'I'm just going to let Doctor Williams know that his patient is here.'

'Carl Adams is here,' Molly said, stepping outside.

'How is he?'

'Not good,' Molly answered. 'We need you here.'

'I'm just in the middle—'

'Luke,' Molly interrupted, 'you accepted a direct admission.'

'His GP said—'

'I don't care what his GP said two hours ago,' Molly said crisply. 'I've got a seriously ill child just landed on my ward, and if he'd gone through Emergency he'd have been triaged to Resus—the emergency doctor would be seeing him, stat. We need you now.'

'I'm on my way.'

'Good,' Molly answered.

'Start him on some nebulised salbutamol.'

'I will, and can you arrange an urgent portable chest X-ray while you're running?'

Anne Marie had already set up the nebuliser. Normally Ventolin was given via a spacer, but Carl's air entry was poor and Molly spoke to Carl's mother as she replaced Carl's oxygen mask with the nebuliser and turned it on.

'Dr Wilson will be here in just a moment, Carl.' Molly helped him lean forward and placed a couple of pillows on his lap. 'Rest on these, that's a good boy. This medicine will start helping soon.' Anne Marie brought over the IV trolley and pulled out some local anaesthetic cream to numb his arm, but Molly shook her head. The cream took a while to work, and there was no point in telling Carl they were giving him cream to numb him before the needle when it wasn't going to have time to take effect.

'Hi, there, Carl.' Luke breezed in and set straight to work, taking a history from the mother as he slipped a tourniquet over Carl's thin arm.

'Carl, I'm just going to put a small needle into your arm. It's going to hurt just a bit, but I'll be as gentle as I can.'

'Are you taking some blood?' Mrs Adams asked.

'Yep, and we can get an IV started and give him some medicine. It will just be the one needle,' Luke reassured them both. 'I'm a pretty good aim.'

He was. Working in paediatrics, he was more than used to the tiny veins of the smallest of babies, but even so Carl barely grimaced as the needle went in, which was worrying. 'We'll need IV hydrocortisone. When did he start his prednisolone?' Luke asked Carl's mother.

'I'm sorry?' Mrs Adams was concentrating on her son.

'Your GP said he started him on a reducing

course of prednisolone on Wednesday. When did he have his last dose? I need to work out how much to give him.'

'Is it really necessary?' Mrs Adams gave an agitated shake of her head. 'He's on the nebuliser. He's already had two courses of steroids in the last couple of months.'

'Mrs Adams.' Luke's voice was calm and even, but there was absolutely no doubt of the seriousness of his question. 'Is your son on the medication your GP prescribed him?'

'He gave me a script and said that if it got worse…' Her voice trailed off for a moment, and Luke did nothing to fill the silence except stare over at the boy struggling to breathe. 'He wasn't like this!' Mrs Adams insisted. 'He actually seemed a bit better, but when he got worse this evening I was going to go and get the prescription dispensed. I don't like him to have steroids. I'm aware what the side effects are.'

Luke didn't even deign to give a response, just called his orders to Molly and administered the essential steroids, all the while talking in reassuring tones to Carl, whose breathing was starting to get a little easier with the cocktail of drugs being delivered via the nebuliser. The radiographer arrived to do a portable X-ray.

'Any chance you could be pregnant?' he asked Molly as he handed her the heavy lead gown. Carl was too ill to be left alone and needed some reassurance and support to sit up and hold his breath while the X-ray was taken.

'No, none,' Molly answered automatically, pulling the heavy gown over her head.

'Actually, I'll stay with him.' Luke took the gown from her. 'Molly, could you ring the nurse-co-ordinator? There aren't any ICU beds. You'll need to let her know that unless he picks up soon, I'm going to have to arrange a transfer.'

It made perfect sense. In fact, transfer or no transfer, she needed an extra nurse out on the ward floor or an experienced nurse to stay with Carl, as his sudden arrival had spread the ward staff thinly and already the routine was falling behind. But Luke had given her a look as she'd taken the gown—just that tiny frown at her carelessness—because until she got her period Luke wouldn't think she was out of the woods.

As Molly headed out of the room there was an uneasy wobble in her throat, a realisation that even if she hadn't outright lied to Luke, she hadn't told the truth.

Hadn't let the man who was closest to her in on the painful truth. It had seemed right at the time—right not to burden him with it.

Only now…

Now somehow she wished that she had.

'Are you OK?' Anne Marie frowned at her pensive face.

'Fine.' Molly nodded, picking up the telephone and putting her personal problems firmly aside.

'This is one sick kid.' Luke's face was grim when he came out of the treatment room. 'What the hell was his mother thinking?'

'I've no idea,' Molly replied. 'I've spoken to the nursing supervisor and she's going to send me a nurse from HDU. Do you still want him to have aminophylline?'

'Not yet.' Luke wrote up his orders on the drug sheet. 'Hopefully he'll start picking up now that he's getting the right medication. For now he needs hourly nebs, but if he doesn't improve soon I'm going to have to transfer him,' Luke said grimly. 'I'm going to talk to the mother.'

'I'll come with you.'

Luke took a long and detailed history from the mother, listening without comment at first when she explained her reasons for not giving the medication.

'He only gets asthma during hay-fever season. Last year they gave him three lots of steroids and this year he's already had two. I just think the doctor hands out the script automatically. I just thought it better to hold off—to see if he improved without them.'

'Why?'

'Because I'm aware of the side-effects.'

'Such as?' Luke frowned.

'Well, it can affect their growth,' Mrs Adams said. 'And Carl's a bit on the short side.'

'Are you aware of the side-effects if he doesn't have them?' Luke asked, and Molly watched Mrs Adams's face tighten. 'Are you aware how sick your son is tonight—that if he doesn't improve in the next couple of hours, or if he deteriorates any further, he's going to have to be transferred to an intensive care bed?'

'I honestly thought I was helping.' Mrs Adams's face crumpled, but Luke's didn't—and because she knew him, Molly knew he was angry. A muscle was leaping in his cheek, his shoulders rigid as he stared coolly at the woman in front of him. 'I just thought if we held off, if I upped his puffers, he'd be OK.'

'If,' Luke said crisply, 'you believe your doctor is over-prescribing, or you don't have faith in him, I suggest you look around for another doctor you can discuss your concerns with, one you feel comfortable with. Do *that*, Mrs Adams, before you start practising internet medicine or testing your theories on your son.'

'I will.' Clearly shaken, Mrs Adams stood up. 'Can I go and sit with him?'

'Of course,' Molly said. 'We're going to keep him in the treatment room for now, where all the equipment is, with a nurse specialling him. I'll take you down to him.'

Luke was still in his office when she came back, his anger still palpable—and he was right to be angry, right to be frustrated, but it was *how* angry he was that concerned Molly. Not white-hot, raging angry, and most wouldn't have even picked up on it, only Molly could feel it.

'Luke—'

'Stupid, stupid woman.' Luke's mouth twisted on the words. 'I don't know whether to report her.'

'She made a mistake,' Molly pointed out.

'And if she makes it again, it could cost her son's life.'

'I think she got that message.'

'What—you think I was too hard on her?'

'No!' Molly shook her head. 'She needed to be told and she was. I don't think she'll play with his health again. But maybe you should discuss it with her GP—or your consultant. Luke…' She was genuinely concerned. They'd sat in this very room with child abusers, had had to listen to the most heinous of things—but his reaction today was extreme. 'Is there something I'm missing here?'

'Like what?' he snapped.

'Well, we all have our buttons,' Molly said slowly, 'and this seems to be yours. Do the twins have asthma?'

'This has nothing to do with the twins, Molly!' Luke glared past her shoulder, then took a deep breath, the anger seeping out of him. 'I'm fine.'

'You're sure?'

'Sure.' He gave a pale smile. 'I'll talk to her again in the morning. I'll go over his asthma plan with her and make sure she's got the message.'

Which he did—only it was Mrs Adams who instigated it.

By seven a.m. Carl was on the main ward, with the nurse special back in her own ward.

'How are you doing?' Luke listened carefully to his chest. 'That sounds a lot better.'

'I feel a lot better.'

'He's tired.' Mrs Adams gave a worried frown. 'He really hasn't slept much.'

'He'll soon catch up on that. We'll probably keep him here over the weekend, just to make sure we're on top of it.'

'Actually, Doctor…' Mrs Adams cleared her throat. 'I was wondering if I could have a word.' She barely got to the ward door before she burst into tears. 'I feel so stupid. I had no idea how bad he'd get.'

'Come on,' Luke said kindly. 'We'll go in my office and have a talk.' He glanced at his watch. 'Er, Molly…'

'No problem.' Molly smiled, but her heart was fluttering at the prospect of meeting his kids. 'I'll keep an eye on them.'

CHAPTER EIGHT

THE office door hadn't even closed before they arrived.

Mrs Williams was holding the twins firmly by the hands, as if she expected them to suddenly run off, as Molly introduced herself.

They were gorgeous.

Blond-haired and blue-eyed, they didn't say a word as Molly led the trio to the playroom. 'You're to sit here and you're not to disturb the staff!' Mrs Williams said sternly to her grand-children, who were sitting on the sofa, both washed and dressed, Amelia with a pair of fairy wings, and little backpacks at their feet and looking just adorable.

Luke was definitely his mother's son—tall, her

blonde hair now streaked with silver, with the strong features that worked better on a male, she was certainly quite a formidable-looking woman, but her eyes were kind.

'I'm terribly sorry to impose!'

'It's not a problem,' Molly assured her, then turned to the twins, who were staring at their feet. 'Your dad's just with a patient at the moment, but he knows that you're here and will try and come along soon. If you need anything, just ask. They'll be fine,' Molly added to the rather anxious Mrs Williams.

'Oh, *they'll* be fine,' Mrs Williams said, after kissing the children and walking with Molly back out to the ward. 'It's your playroom I'm worried about! They may look as if butter wouldn't melt but they can be a couple of little minxes. They're way too used to running wild.'

Which Molly doubted—Luke was so insistent on respect and good manners, and Molly could now see where it came from. Mrs Williams really was an imposing woman and no doubt ran a tight ship. 'Again, I really do apologise for the inconvenience.'

'Happens all the time!' Molly said cheerfully, walking her out of the ward. Well, maybe not *all* the time, but a staff member's child sitting in the playroom, waiting for their parent to finish their shift wasn't a unique occurrence on the children's ward, though usually it was their mother they were waiting for, and that fact alone meant that the staff would give them just a little bit more fuss than usual.

'What are they like?' Anne Marie asked, coming out of the kitchen with a baby bottle.

'Gorgeous,' Molly said. 'Come and say hi!'

Only the two little angels she'd left sitting not two minutes ago seemed to have left the building—toys were everywhere, the television blaring, Amelia jumping up and down on the sofa as Angus sped around on a tricycle that was way too small for him.

'Hey, guys…' Anne Marie barked over the noise of the television. 'Time to settle down.'

'You talk funny!' Amelia giggled, jumping up and down on the sofa. 'Doesn't she, Angus?'

'Yeah.' Angus zoomed the tricycle to a stop. 'You talk funny!'

'Gorgeous!' Anne Marie rolled her eyes. 'And such lovely manners, too!'

Anne Marie, in fact, ended up feeding her patient in the playroom so she could keep an eye on the twins. The other nurses watched the ward while Molly gave handover to the day staff, which took for ever as Rita had been off for two days and didn't know most of the patients.

'How's Bernadette's mood?'

'She's perked up,' Molly said. 'She's getting on well with young Nathan, so she's got a friend now, but it's the school disco this weekend, apparently—she really feels she's missing out.'

'She is missing out,' Rita sighed. 'She's been here for weeks now.'

'And that one!' Anne Marie was giving her orders, and the playroom was a lot tidier by the time Molly came back. 'Go on, put it back in the toy box!'

'Ready for the off?' Molly grinned.

'Am I ever. I just want to ring John before I go, though— Oh, hi, Luke.'

'Daddy!' Two squeals of delight went up and the twins hurled themselves at him.

'How have they been?' Luke asked. 'Not too much trouble, I hope?'

'They were great.' Anne Marie beamed through gritted teeth. 'Full of beans!'

'Well, thank you.' Luke gripped the twins' hands tightly as he headed off, and this time Molly knew why. With Anne Marie ringing her husband, Molly walked out with Luke.

'How was Mrs Adams?' Molly asked.

'Good.' Luke nodded. 'I've handed it over to Tom, and I'm sure it won't happen again—she just didn't realise how serious it could get. I've gone over everything with her, and in fairness I don't think her GP really had explained things very well. She had no real idea about peak-flow recordings and how important they were.' Luke held onto the twins rather than smother the loud yawn that hit him.

'Are you going to get any sleep?'

'Nope…' Luke yawned again. 'Not till Mum gets back from her appointment.'

'What about kinder?' Molly asked, then answered her own question. 'Oh, that's right, they don't have it on Friday. Will you be OK for work tonight?'

'I'll have to be!'

'Luke…' They were at the car park, his eyes so red it looked as if he'd been swimming in chlorine. She actually opened her mouth to offer to come over and watch them till his mum got back. After all, she didn't have to work tonight—it made perfect sense, what any friend would do…

'What?' He was holding two little hands in one big one as he fumbled in his pocket for his car keys.

'Oh, nothing… See you, then.'

'See you, Molly.'

'See you, guys!'

And it was as much of a goodbye as they could have with the twins there. Only it hurt, actually felt wrong to be walking away when she didn't want to. To know she wouldn't see Luke till Monday, to know he was exhausted and she could do something to help.

But that meant crossing the line.

That meant getting involved.

And that was something she *needed* to think carefully about.

There was nothing as bleak as a post-divorce birthday.

There was nothing as bleak as letting yourself in at five minutes past midnight to a house that was empty and a husband that was no longer there.

Oh, she'd been a sister doing it for herself tonight, had wiggled her bum on the dance floor and sworn she'd survive along with the rest of the crowd.

And she would.

Holding her cat to her chest, even though he was

scratching to get out, Molly knew that she would survive. Glimpsed that day in the long way-off future, when she'd bump into Richard and his rapidly growing brood and be able to smile.

Molly stared at the wall, at the silly crystals she'd hung to promote new energy, held onto her cat, who was purring now, and hated it that she was alone on her birthday.

It wasn't age she feared, and it wasn't loneliness—just that horrible thought that you might die in bed alone. Unnoticed for days. That you weren't worth checking on, Molly thought melodramatically. But it was ten minutes into her birthday so she was allowed to be, Molly decided, because next year she'd be thirty.

Which had her reaching for the tissues.

And she knew people cared. Molly blew loudly into her tissue.

She knew she'd be missed before the neighbours noticed a pong.

Rolling on her side, Molly hugged her cat closer. She knew that she mattered.

Only it wasn't the same.

'Good that there aren't kids involved.'

Everyone said it—her lawyer, her family, her friends, even Luke.

And she wasn't being melodramatic any more, just very, very sad and terribly honest…

With herself.

Because, yes, she smiled and nodded, almost right to the point she agreed—only this horrible, selfish part of her didn't.

She *wanted* there to have been kids involved and pictures on her fridge, to be yawning at work because the kids wouldn't let her sleep, wanted to moan that her boobs were no more. Was sick of working over Christmas because apparently she didn't need to be home on Christmas morning.

But she wanted to be there so badly that it really was a need.

A need Richard had had too—a need that had pushed Molly to look at adoption.

But he'd wanted his own children, which meant that he hadn't wanted her—and she didn't want him any more either. She wanted Luke—only she didn't want his kids…

'Why do men snore?' Anne-Marie's warm Scottish voice on the end of the phone pierced her loneliness.

'Why does every man I fall in love with go and get someone else pregnant?'

'There's no answer to either,' Anne Marie sighed. 'I rang a few times, so don't think you've got a load of messages! Oh, and I've decided that we're getting next-door flats in the retirement village,' she continued, pretending she couldn't hear her friend's tears. "We'll drink lots of gin and cheat at bingo and you can flirt with all the rich retirees!'

'I'm not worried about getting old.'

'Well, I am, and just in case you are, I'm letting you know that we've got a plan! Happy birthday, Molly.'

CHAPTER NINE

'HAPPY birthday!'

Blinking at her front door, her dressing-gown wrapped around her, Molly tried to work out what day it was.

She'd been out with friends last night, Friday night, and then Anne Marie had rung. Luke had been working, but he was off for the weekend now...which meant it was Saturday morning, Molly realised.

And she was still alive!

Very early in the morning, actually, and Luke was standing in her doorway, dressed in scrubs, in desperate need of a shave and holding...

'Here!' He handed her a massive bunch of flowers—not roses, which was good, because they weren't her favourite. Instead he'd brought a massive bunch of pale pink lilies, which *were* her favourite—especially when they came with lots of carefully arranged twigs sticking out, especially when they were being held out by a gorgeous specimen of a man.

'I'm assuming you didn't get these at the local garage.' Molly buried her face in them and no doubt came out with a yellow nose. 'And I don't think the local florist opens at…' Glancing at the oven clock, she did a double take. 'Six a.m.! Luke, what on earth are you doing here?'

'I asked Tom to come in early.'

'Why?'

'Why do you think, Molly? It's your birthday—I feel awful that I can't take you out tonight.'

'Well, don't,' Molly said firmly. 'And don't listen to what Anne Marie says either—you need some time with the twins and you can't keep asking your mum. I mean, it's fine for work and everything, but…' Her voice sort of trailed off.

'You know, I think she'd actually be pleased if I told her I was seeing someone.'

'You haven't told her, then.' Molly's cheeks were pink because she hadn't told her family either. She certainly wasn't going to tell her parents, who'd no doubt get ahead of themselves, who'd no doubt start giving knowing little smiles and assuming it was something serious…

Which it wasn't.

'What would I tell her?' came his pertinent reply, but he didn't wait for her answer. 'Breakfast?' he said instead, holding out a greasy-looking bag.

'Croissants?' Molly said hopefully.

'*Chocolate* croissants,' Luke said proudly. 'You go back to bed and I'll bring it in.'

So she did. Happily followed doctor's orders. After a quick brush of her teeth and a few squirts of perfume, oh, and a very quick comb of her hair, plus the teeniest bit of body lotion and a very quick tidy of her room, Molly hopped back in and had arranged the sheet around her, just enough to show a bit of cleavage, just in time to pretend she'd been there for ages, when Luke came in with a tray heaped with coffee and croissants, which Molly fell on.

'Climb in.' She grinned. 'There's plenty of room.'

'Better not.'

'Don't be shy, now.' Molly smiled.

'I've only got till eight…'

'Plenty of time, then,' Molly joked, but her smile faded when she saw the strained look on his face.

'Look, Molly, I didn't come here for that.' She felt stupid all of a sudden, like some raving nymphomaniac, felt stupid and embarrassed, and not even a bite of delectable chocolate croissant could take away the sting of his words. 'I came to see you. I wanted to see you because it's your birthday.'

'I know.'

'Do you?' Luke pinned her with his eyes, then he closed them, let out the longest breath as Molly held hers. 'Do you understand that I didn't come here just to get you into bed? I'm exhausted, Mol,' he said, reverting for the first time to the name he'd once called her. 'Trying to squeeze everything in—kinder, the twins, work, us…'

'You didn't come here to dump me…' Molly tried a brave smile '…again?'

'Yeah.' Luke rolled his eyes and smiled back. 'I came here to dump you on your birthday! I'm just trying to…' He faltered as he tried and failed to find the words. 'I'm sorry, Molly, my intention was to cheer you up, not spread my misery. Sometimes it would be nice just to be…to do…I don't know… Angus is having nightmares. I ought to be there for him at night. It's not fair on my mum either. I'm snatching a couple of hours' sleep here and there, you know, waking to pick them up from kinder and give them lunch, then back to bed, then up to give them dinner and their bath. I just don't feel I'm giving any area of my life the attention it needs and I know for a fact I'm not giving you the attention you deserve.'

'You're being a bit hard on yourself,' Molly offered. 'Things will settle down.'

'I know. I've got this interview in a couple of weeks.' He ran an exasperated hand over his forehead. 'If I get it, my hours will be more civilised, and the twins start school in a few months. Mum's been great helping with them. If we can just muddle through till then…'

'Things will get easier,' Molly said gently. 'I mean, it's only been a few months since…' She gave a little tight shrug. 'You've had a big move. The kids starting a new kinder, you starting a new job…'

'You.'

'Me.' Molly nodded. 'We're supposed to be about making things better for each other, Luke, not harder.'

'You don't,' Luke said firmly. 'God, Molly, if you knew how much I looked forward to our time together, how nice it feels to just be me for a while. I'm not trying to end things, I'm just trying to explain. I want you more in my life, I don't want it to be transient, some little secret. I'm not asking for for ever, I know you don't want to get too involved, but I want us to do normal things.'

'We do do normal things,' Molly attempted.

'Like have dinner together?' Luke offered.

'How can we? We both work nights and on the nights you're off…'

'I'm not asking you to stay over at my place,' Luke said. 'I know that would be too confusing for the kids, but, hell, can't we just be friends—at least to them? I don't know, my head's all over the place.' He gave a defeated shrug. 'I guess I just need to—'

'Sleep?' Molly offered, watching a watery smile lighten his tired face.

'Yeah—and wake up for once,' Luke said, 'with you.'

'Climb in, then,' Molly said again, only this time it was said without a trace of innuendo. Placing the tray on her bedside table, she set the alarm for eight as Luke peeled off his theatre blues and clambered in beside her. 'You've got an hour and forty-five minutes.' She kissed his mouth as he groaned in pleasure at the prospect of sleep. 'Now, close your eyes and make the most of it.'

'God, Molly,' Luke said, pulling her into the crook of his arm and lying back on the pillow, 'you know exactly how to please…'

He didn't even finish what he was saying. He was out like a light in mid-sentence and Molly lay for a good five minutes, her head on his chest, feeling the rise and fall of his breathing. Her flimsy cheap curtains were a bargain at twice the price, because they allowed in enough light for her to see the contours of his body, the smatter of hair on his chest, the way it swirled round his nipples like water going down a plughole, flat, hard nipples that she ached to touch but wouldn't.

Wriggling out of his arm, Molly propped herself up on her elbow and stared down at him, realising that even asleep he looked exhausted, his face still tense, his mouth tightly closed, as if on permanent guard. Pushing aside her own hurt, pushing aside the blame, and the reasons, she actually tried to see how it must be for him. Working five nights a week, his mother ill, trying to raise troubled twins and grieving himself, too—surely, even if they were just lovers, even if this was ultimately going nowhere, they were friends too.

And friends helped each other when needed.

Curling up, she faced the wall, felt him stir behind her, felt him spoon against her, safe in the cocoon of his arms, safe and peaceful for a little while longer in the world that they had created, half dozing and half dreading the buzz of the alarm that would shatter it, wondering if she could spare it—spare just a tiny bit more of *that* piece without leaving herself open to hurt. It wasn't the alarm but instead Luke's kiss that roused her. He lifted her hair and slowly, slowly kissed the back of her neck as thoroughly as if it were her mouth, the arm that was over her drawing her closer, warm lazy skin on warm lazy skin as his hand softly kneaded her breast.

'I've been thinking—'

'No thinking,' Luke interrupted his kiss just long enough to respond. 'It's your birthday.'

And back he went, back to where her neck met her shoulders, his tongue caressing her, his teeth nibbling her tender flesh as the arm that was beneath her moved lower, his hand coming to rest a teasing moment between the soft warmth of her legs. She could hear his breath on her ear as he shifted himself slightly, knew, because she knew him, that his eyes were closed, that he was savouring each sensation as much as her, his fingers sliding to her most intimate place now, his gorgeous erection just there at her entrance. Only the birthday girl wasn't in any rush, just revelling in the bliss of this man who knew her body, this man who could read every little moan and get it absolutely right. And it was rude to compare performances, Molly thought, purring like a kitten as he stroked her deeper, and she never ever would, Molly gasped, as the pressure grew more insistent. It would be like trying to choose between chocolate or strawberry milkshake, she decided, biting on her lip as his ragged breathing matched hers, Richard strawberry, Luke chocolate…

'Luke…' She didn't actually say it, this sort of urgent mental plea that he'd already answered on entering.

God, how did he do it? Molly wondered, because from the outside they were barely moving, yet from the inside, each deep, measured thrust, had her frenzied, until she could take it no more—shuddering in his still busy hand as he shuddered deep within her, as still he kissed her neck, as her head swung round to capture his mouth, the question begged again—how did he do it? How did he always, always just know how?

The alarm clock blared its applause as they arrived just ahead of schedule, and it beat its electronic tune for a minute or two before they managed to move.

'I've been thinking…' Molly attempted again, now that she could actually focus her thoughts, and focus she did, just for a second, just for a quick last-minute check with her brain before she turned and opened her mouth. 'Why don't I pop over this afternoon, just for an hour? I'm going to Mum's for my birthday dinner. I could stop by on the way, say hi to the twins.'

He didn't say anything, just stared back at her.

'And if I drop by now and then, well, in a couple of weeks maybe they'll be OK with me picking them up from kinder now and then.'

'You're sure?' Luke frowned. 'But you said—'

'That I didn't want to be involved. That I didn't want to be Daddy's girlfriend—but I *am* your friend, Luke.'

'If we keep it light.' There was relief in his voice and something else too. 'Just a friend dropping in. What sort of thing would you drop by Anne Marie's for?'

Molly gave a helpless shrug. 'I don't really need a reason to drop by—I just text her and tell her to put the kettle on or to pour me a glass of wine.'

'Maybe you could be lending me a DVD?'

'OK.' Molly nodded, because it sounded like a sort of plan.

'And then you'll stay for coffee?'

'Sure,' Molly said, 'or maybe a milkshake.'

'Milkshake.' His head on the pillow jerked towards hers and he frowned at her odd response, then with a quick kiss he climbed out of bed, grimaced at the clock and started to get dressed. 'I'm sure I can rustle some up—what flavour do you like?'

'I can't say,' Molly squeaked.

'What?'

'Well, I can,' Molly gulped. 'Actually, I know full well which one I prefer—I just feel really guilty saying it!'

'What are you talking about, Molly?' He dug in his pocket and pulled out a little box, his voice a bit gruff when next he spoke. 'Here—happy birthday.'

He'd wrapped it too—and she tore at the paper, no gentle shaking or a moment pretending to guess. Instead, she gleefully pulled off the paper, muttering something about how he shouldn't have, but clearly delighted that he had. Her eyes were shining as brightly as the silver pendant and looked up to thank him, seeing him standing there, her body still thrumming from his attention, this birthday so unlike last year's, this birthday such a happy one. And even if Luke wouldn't understand the compliment he was being given, she gave it anyway.

'Chocolate milkshake,' Molly said firmly, watching his eyes crinkle in confusion, not just at the strange response to a gift but at the little surreptitious smile on her lips. 'I by far prefer chocolate.'

'Chocolate it is, then.' He kissed the tip of her nose.

'And I don't feel guilty for saying it—not in the least.'

'Good for you!' He kissed her mouth then let her go. 'You crazy lady!'

CHAPTER TEN

'HI!' MOLLY beamed. 'Here…that DVD you said you wanted.' Thrusting one of her many chick flicks at Luke, Molly stood in the hall as four blue eyes peered at her from the staircase.

Six, actually, if you counted the rather large photo of Amanda on the wall!

'Oh, hi, Molly.' He was giving his political speech again. 'Thank you for that. I'm sure I'll enjoy watching it. Kids, this is Molly, a friend from work. She's a nurse.'

'We already met.' Molly smiled. 'The other morning.'

Still they stood there, staring.

'And she's just lending me a DVD I've been

wanting to watch. You'll stay for a drink, won't you?'

'Love to!' Molly answered as four little eyes narrowed to slits.

'My mum was a doctor.' Amelia stood on the stairs, a little angel with her fluffy blonde hair and little pink nightdress and still with those very faded fairy wings on, but Molly could have sworn she had horns as her eyes narrowed at their surprise guest. 'Daddy,' sang her cherubic little voice, 'a doctor's much better than a nurse, isn't it?'

'It's different,' Luke said, leading Molly through to the kitchen, as the children brought up the rear. 'It's a different job—and different is good.'

'Why?' Angus joined his sister—ooh, next to *another* photo of Amanda. 'Why is different good?'

'It just is.' Luke shrugged. 'Who's for a chocolate milkshake?'

'I like your wings,' Molly offered, shrinking in

her chair as Amelia simultaneously smiled and hexed her with her eyes.

'Mummy bought them for me.'

'Come on, Amelia.' Angus picked up his drink and so did his sister. 'Let's go.'

'I don't want to.' Amelia replied, sitting herself down at the table, like a little judge with her chocolate milk moustache. 'I want to stay and talk to Molly.'

Not that she said a word.

Didn't offer a 'Happy birthday' when Luke told her that it was, just scribbled in her colouring book, refusing any attempt by Molly or Luke to include her in the conversation.

'Cute,' Molly croaked when finally Amelia wandered off to join her brother. 'They're really cute.'

'They're not really used to people dropping in.' Luke ran a hand through his hair and let out a long breath. 'Since we've been here in Melbourne, well, it's really only been family.'

'As Angus said, they don't like different,'

Molly said calmly, but she was wearing her nurse's hat more than her own. 'And I guess, with what they've been through….'

'They've been through an awful lot.' Something in his voice made her start, something in Luke's voice was so urgent, so raw she nearly slopped her milkshake. 'An awful lot.' He shook his head, painted on a smile as the twins ambled back, and Molly drank up just as quickly as she could.

'I'd better get going.' Molly glanced at her watch. 'Mum will be expecting me.'

'Well, have a great night. Say bye to Molly, guys.'

'See you.' Molly gave a wide smile, though her jaw was aching, and when no response was forthcoming, when they didn't even turn their heads, she put a hand up to stop him as Luke called to his children again to say goodbye.

'It's fine,' she said, having to stop herself from mewing to be let out as Luke saw her to the door.

'I'm sure it'll get easier.'

'Of course it will,' Molly said, only she wasn't so sure—wasn't sure at all.

'So you've met the twins?' Anne Marie closed the door and didn't even pretend to walk over to check the drugs.

'A couple of times.' Molly tried to keep her voice light.

'I thought you'd both decided to leave them out of it.'

'We did,' Molly said, chewing on her bottom lip. 'We are. Look, I'm not going to stay over or anything. I'm just a friend from work—helping out a bit—like yesterday he was stuck in Emergency with a sick baby, and his mum needed him home on time because she had to go to the doctor. Now, if the twins knew me a bit better, I could have gone over and taken them to kinder.'

'That's not leaving them out of it,' Anne Marie pointed out.

'It isn't,' Molly gulped, 'but I trust myself to do the right thing by the twins, and Luke trusts me too. And whatever happens or doesn't happen between us, we've agreed that we'll stay friends, so I'm not going to suddenly disappear.'

'Because they've had enough of that,' Anne Marie said sternly, 'with their mother and everything.'

'This isn't about introducing me into their lives,' Molly said firmly. 'This is about me helping Luke out because, sadly it isn't a perfect world, and it sucks that he's a single dad, working nights and trying to raise twins. And friends help with things like that.'

'They do.' Anne Marie nodded. 'Molly, I trust you too, I know you're going to do the right thing by the twins, and that's what's worrying me. On every level you're involved now, and I'm worried that you're the one who's going to get hurt.'

'Not again,' Molly said firmly. 'I've toughened right up. I know what I'm doing, Anne Marie.'

'But do you? Molly, you're…' She stopped herself saying it, and there was this horrible gap—Anne Marie opening her mouth to speak, then changing her mind, then giving her friend a smile. 'So? What are they like at home?' Anne Marie asked, only Molly was sure that wasn't what she had been about to say.

'Awful!' Molly actually giggled, just so relieved to be able to talk about it—so nice to be honest. 'I know they're as cute as buttons to look at, but they're the rudest, cheekiest little things. And you should see the way Luke is with them, *nothing* like he is at work.'

'What do you mean?'

'Well, he's lovely to the kids here, but he is pretty stern with them.'

'He does like good manners.'

'Not from his own kids, though. Honestly, he needs to discipline them!'

'Careful!' Anne Marie grinned. 'You're starting to sound like a wicked stepmother.'

'Perish the thought.' Molly shuddered.

'Honestly, Anne Marie, you don't have to worry about me getting too involved. There's no way I'd take that little lot on.'

'I had visitors today,' Bernadette said once Molly had given her IVs and checked the dressing on her leg and rearranged her pillows. 'Some of my friends from school, and Carly and Marcus came, too.'

'That was nice.'

'It was.' Bernadette grinned and spoke in an excited whisper. 'And Carly was trying to chat to…' She wagged a thumb at the closed curtain. 'And he didn't even answer her. Then he asked Carly to pass the TV guide to me, so we could choose what movie to watch tonight!'

'Fab!' Molly grinned.

'How did you feel about *Marcus*?' She mouthed the last word.

'He was annoying.' Bernadette blinked. 'He kept going on about his stupid football, and he was all proud because he'd got in trouble with the principal—I mean, like it's something to be pleased about!'

'I hear you had some other good news today!' Molly wasn't surprised when Bernadette's face fell a touch.

'I go home in two days.' Bernadette attempted a smile. 'I can't wait. Are you working tomorrow?'

'I'm off,' Molly said. 'I'm off now for five nights.'

'So I won't see you again?'

'You might—I do go shopping. Who knows?' She tried to keep her voice light, but this was the hard bit—when someone you were genuinely fond of, when someone you'd come to really like, was ready to go home. Though she was pleased and thrilled for Bernadette, Molly would miss her too. 'Maybe you could pop back for a little visit near Christmas, let us see what you look like in real clothes.'

'Can I ring the ward and make sure you're working?'

'Of course you can.' Molly smiled. 'Are you a bit nervous?'

'Why would I be nervous about going home?'

'A lot of people are,' Molly said. 'It's very normal to feel nervous and anxious about going home after such a long time in hospital—as well as excited!'

'Really?'

'Really!' Molly nodded.

'I'm worried about school,' Bernadette admitted. 'I know everyone's been in to see me and I've tried to keep up with my work, but it's just going to be weird.'

'For a little while probably,' Molly said, 'but you'll settle in soon and the teachers will understand if you're a bit behind.'

'It's not just that…'

'Hey, Bernadette!' Nathan's voice, on the verge of breaking, squeaked then became baritone from behind the curtain. 'That movie you were talking about—it's being shown in the holidays!'

'Is it?'

'I should be out by then!' Behind the curtain Molly and Bernadette bit their knuckles, eyes wide in anticipation. 'Maybe we should go…'

'What do I say?' Bernadette mouthed frantically.

'Yes!' Molly mouthed back, urgently nodding her head.

'If you want to.' Nathan attempted nonchalance.

'Cool!' Bernadette said, high-fiving Molly. 'Sounds good!'

'So what was that other problem you were going to tell me about?' Molly grinned. 'Or am I right in thinking that it's just been sorted?'

'What will I wear?' Bernadette whispered.

'We'll think of something!'

'Guess what?' Looking as happy as Bernadette, Luke shouted to Molly as she walked past the doctor's office. 'I'm a free man!'

'What are you talking about?'

'Close the door!'

There was something different about him, something she couldn't pinpoint.

'I've slept for ten hours straight!' Luke grinned, as if reading her thoughts, and so too did Molly. *That* was the difference—he wasn't ragged with exhaustion. 'I feel great.'

'Fantastic!'

'That's not the good news.' He pulled at her waist, pulled her right in as Molly tried to wriggle away.

'Luke…not here.'

'The door's closed.'

'I don't care.'

'OK, then.' Reluctantly, he let her go. 'Mum's taken the twins to her sister's. They're away for two nights! Should I feel guilty that I'm so pleased?'

'No.' Molly laughed. 'You should hear Anne Marie singing when hers go to her mum's!'

It was as five years had been wiped away—the stupid little games they'd played, the silly things he did, made her do, that had made her laugh remembered again, her lips twitching as, so scarily easily, they reverted to the ways of old.

'Say please,' Luke said.

'Please, what, Luke?'

'Please, will you take me out somewhere really fabulous tomorrow night?' Luke grinned.

'You're working tomorrow!'

'Not any more—I arranged Tom to cover for me. I want to take you out.'

'But you need to save your days off,' Molly pointed out. 'If your mum's not well, surely you should work when you've got the chance. You might need Tom to cover for you next week.'

'Don't even try to make me feel guilty. I haven't had a night out in…' He dragged a hand through his hair '…I don't know in how long. And I haven't been to a restaurant that doesn't have a kids' menu in ages…and I'm sick of sponging off you. I'm taking you out and you're staying at my place. So say please.'

'Please, what?' Molly attempted a sigh, but it was hard with lips that were grinning.

'Please, Luke, will you buy me loads of lovely cocktails and then have your wicked way with me?'

'OK,' she relented. 'Please, will you take me out—somewhere fabulous—buy me lots of cocktails and then have your wicked way with me?'

'Seeing as you asked so nicely!' Luke grinned. 'And make sure you wear something nice!'

Regretting her rather glib response to Bernadette's question, Molly debated it with Anne Marie long into the night.

'Buy something!' Anne Marie urged as Molly went to answer a bell. 'Something sexy and slinky that will knock his socks off!'

And she would have bought something had she not again slept through her alarm!

Hair dripping, leg bleeding from a hasty shave, she eyed the contents of her wardrobe! So far, Luke had seen her in jeans, or nurse's uniform, or jeans… Molly sighed. She literally hadn't got a thing to wear. Richard had spent the last couple of years of their marriage taking her temperature to see if she was ovulating rather than taking her out—and she hadn't exactly been kicking up her heels since the break-up. What the hell was she going to wear? Jumping when her doorbell rang, shot with nerves, Molly let out a moan of horror. Surely he couldn't be that early.

'Oh, it's you!' Which sounded not much of a greeting, but never had she been so pleased to see her friend.

'Bearing champagne and a little black number!' Anne Marie handed a bag to Molly. 'And hair product. I knew you'd oversleep!'

'It's gorgeous…' Molly pulled the tiniest dress out of the tiniest bag, black, velvety and just superb, but she shook her head when she put it on. 'It's too much!'

'It's not too much! I bought that dress in the hope I'd slim into it. God, if I looked like that in it, I'd be wearing it to the shops! You look fantastic!'

She did—well, sort of. Molly could see that.

All boobs and bum, but sort of sophisticated too, and, as Anne Marie had predicted, it would knock Luke's socks off.

'I'll think about it,' Molly said.

'You could always wear your jeans!' Anne Marie pointed out.

Sipping champagne, Molly closed her eyes and tried to relax as Anne Marie set to work on her make-up.

'Not too much!' Molly warned.

'Why not?' Anne Marie asked. 'Oh, that's right, you don't want him to think you've gone to any effort!"

'Not too much of an effort!' Molly agreed.

'Because you're not having a relationship or anything…' Anne Marie nattered on as she lengthened Molly's eyelashes with mascara. 'I mean, you can hardly keep your hands off each other, he's moving heaven and earth to take you out tonight, you're both grinning like idiots whenever you see each other and you're ferrying his kids…'

Ouch.

Unwittingly, perhaps, Anne Marie had hit on a surprisingly raw nerve.

The occasional favour she'd been up for seemed to be morphing into something else. A kinder run here, a quick half-hour there—their worlds were sort of merging, only Molly wasn't at all sure it was for all the right reasons.

'You think he's using me?' Brave with her eyes closed, she asked her friend the question.

'No,' Anne Marie answered—only she took just a second too long. 'I like Luke—he's gorgeous and it's clear that he adores you.'

'But.'

'Have you heard about your course?' Molly's eyes flicked open, because she was sure that wasn't what Anne Marie had been going to say.

'It will be a couple of weeks yet. Tell me, Anne Marie, do you think he's using me?'

'Don't be daft.' Anne Marie smiled, picking up her tongs and setting to work on her friend's hair. 'You just go out and have a good night—heaven knows, you deserve it.'

She did! Even Molly knew that, and there was no reason not to have a good time.

No work, no alarm clocks, no Angus and Amelia to take up their time—just the two of them.

'Done!'

'Oh, my goodness!' Molly stared back at her reflection. Her wild curls for once were tamed and glossy, she had lashings of mascara on smoky grey eyes and her mouth, pale and glossy, broke into a nervous giggle. 'I look…' She tried to find the word—not tarty, not overdone, just fab!

'God help Luke!' Anne Marie giggled.

Anne Marie had barely driven off when Luke's car appeared, and, feeling as nervous as she had on their first date, *more* nervous than she had on their first date, Molly opened the door.

'Hi, there…' He gave her a tight smile. 'You look nice.'

'Thanks!' Molly smiled, more than a touch deflated by his response. 'So do you.'

He did. He didn’t usually wear a suit, but he was wearing one now, and wearing it well—those long limbs longer somehow, those green eyes greener against the slate of his tie. And he smelt…Molly could feel her insides wobble a bit as she caught a whiff of his cologne.

‘We’d better go.’ He looked down at his watch. “The table’s booked for eight.’

‘Sure.’ Molly thought her face would crack from smiling, hating how awkward it all was. ‘I’ve just got to feed the cat!’

How, Luke asked himself, could she make feeding the cat sexy? But there she was, boobs spilling out over her dress as she bent down, the cat mewing round her feet, feet that were wrapped in high, strappy heels…

‘Hurry up, Molly.’

‘I am!’

He didn’t want to take her out, Molly decided. He hadn’t even kissed her when he’d come in. All the old doubts were back, tears pricking her eyes as she bent over to get her bag and check she had her phone and lipstick. What the hell were they going to talk about? A whole night, no kids, no buzzers, no sex to distract them…

'Come on, Molly,' Luke urged, practically marching her to the door.

'You don't want to go, do you?' Molly halted at the final hurdle.

'What are you talking about?'

'You haven't even kissed me!'

'What?'

'You're worried what we'll talk about!'

'Believe me!' Luke shook his head. 'That's not the problem!'

'Then what is?'

'Molly…' He closed his eyes in frustration. 'I want you to have a good night. I'm well aware what an utter louse I am at taking you out. I spoke to Anne Marie…'

'Uh-oh!'

'She said I shouldn't lay a finger on you, should

take you somewhere nice…which I'm about to. Only she didn't know I'd turn up to find you…'

'She got me ready…' Molly giggled. 'I told you, she's a witch!'

'A good witch, though.' Luke grinned.

'She's probably sipping champagne and cackling with laughter at this very minute,' Molly said, picturing it for a moment then promptly forgetting about Anne Marie. 'So you do want to ravish me?'

'God, yes…' Luke groaned, kissing her throat so as not to spoil her make-up. 'And you do want to be ravished?'

'God, yes,' Molly whimpered, fiddling with his zip as his hands pushed up her dress, 'but the table's booked for eight.'

'I'll be quick,' Luke gasped, encountering the briefest, sexiest of knickers. 'Don't worry about that!'

He'd returned in stages—in the weeks since he'd been back, it was as if she'd glimpsed parts of the Luke of old. Sexy Luke. Angry Luke. Funny Luke. Her Luke. But only in parts. But tonight he was back.

All of him.

All of the man she had once so dearly loved.

And all of the *them* they had once been.

He took her to a very nice Asian restaurant, which was Molly's favourite, got her tipsy on Singapore slings as they worked their way through the menu—sharing dishes, eating aromatic sweet curries and cooling their tongues on hunks of watermelon, devouring slabs of beef rib with coriander and ginger then gorging on the sweetest rice pudding, and not once, not even for a second, was it uncomfortable.

Speaking about everything and nothing.

Not the kids or the past, just where they were now and the future, not a single sticky moment as they somehow got back to how they had been.

Massaged each other's egos and made each other feel better, as they had both promised they would.

And it felt so nice to sit with the only guy in

the world who didn't care if she had something on her teeth.

Because, when she inevitably did, he merely told her.

And Molly merely wiped it off.

'You're driving!' Molly reminded him as he ordered two Singapore slings this time.

'Not tonight.'

So they abandoned the car and headed for a stylish bar.

Walking along the river to get there, even though it was midnight it was as busy as if it were the middle of the day, but it was only about the two of them.

They paused to stare into the designer shop windows as Molly oohed and ahhed at the handbags, in absolutely no hurry to head home.

They enjoyed more delicious cocktails as Molly smouldered on her stool and blew kisses at Luke, then they snogged in the taxi all the way to his home.

And she was a bit more than tipsy, Molly

realised as she brushed her teeth in his bathroom, which was no way to behave on a first date.

Only it wasn't their first, Molly consoled herself.

And it wasn't really a date. Molly hiccoughed.

But it was.

One of those lovely, lovely dates where you don't have to impress because you know that you do.

Teetering into his bedroom, she braced herself for a zillion photos of her nemesis, frowning just a touch when she realised there wasn't even one!

Not that she had time to dwell on it.

It was a night so perfect that when her head was spinning too much to bend down, a very well-oiled Luke even took off her shoes.

'Good night?' Luke checked as he bundled her into bed.

'You know that it was.'

A night so perfect that when he climbed in beside her and held her, Molly never wanted it to end. And no matter how much she tried to deny it, as those hands held her, as his mouth

CHAPTER ELEVEN

'CAN I talk to you?' Despite the early hour, despite the fact she was on her side and facing away from him, Molly knew he was awake, had felt him restless beside her for the last hour or so, and she didn't want the morning to come, didn't want to have to face the consequences of last night's closeness—almost knew what was coming before he'd even spoken, could feel his hand on her shoulder, for once tentative. 'About Amanda?'

'Not now.'

'I have to, Molly…' He paused for a moment and she knew what was coming—stared at the curtains as he turned the knife… 'When I left you, there was something I didn't tell you. I'd found out that she was pregnant.'

'Molly?' When she didn't say anything, when she didn't move or turn over, Luke pressed for a response, but all she could manage was to push away his hand. 'Molly, say something.'

'What am I supposed to say, Luke?' Her voice was as bitter as she felt. '"Oh, well, that's all right, then? Thanks for explaining!"?'

'I had to give it a chance to work.'

'Well, good for you.'

'Molly, I'm trying to tell you why I left you.'

'You really think I hadn't worked it out? For God's sake, Luke, I'm not stupid. The twins were born five months after we broke up. It's not just why you left me, it's how you left me—how you left us!' She couldn't deal with this, really couldn't deal with this, and, ripping back the sheets, she jumped out of bed, scrabbling on the floor for her clothes. 'You know, you really should get off your moral high horse. How dare you stand waving antibiotics at me and telling me as a nurse I should know better?' She spat the words at him. 'You were two doctors, Luke. Two doctors who should have known better before they messed up my life.' And because her car was at her place and his was in the city, she had to stand shivering in her own misery as she waited for a taxi.

'Don't go racing off.' He stood in the hall beside her, the outburst that had had to happen fading a touch.

'I'm not racing off, Luke.' She even managed a pale smile at his questioning look. 'Well, I was but I'm not now. I actually want to go into work and see Bernadette this morning. She's being discharged, and I want to pop in and say goodbye.'

'When did you get so nice?'

'I've always been nice,' Molly said, lowering her eyes, only not quickly enough that he missed the flash of tears.

'I know you have—and you didn't deserve to be treated the way you were.'

'No, I didn't.'

'Molly! If we're ever going to move on, we

need to deal with this. I guess the question is do you want to?'

'Can't we keep things as they are?' And it was a pointless question because since he'd came back into her life nothing had stayed the same for a single moment—everything galloping forward, no matter how hard she tried to pull back.

'You know we can't,' Luke said, and when she didn't say anything back, Luke did—rammed in the knife and twisted her own guilt this time a bit further. 'I'm sorry I came on so strong about the antibiotics—guilty as charged to double standards. I was worried for you, that's all.'

'For me?' Molly let out a soft, mocking laugh. 'Sure you were.'

'Molly, my life couldn't get much more chaotic now. What's another unplanned baby?' He was joking, she knew that, only it hurt too much to joke about, especially with what came next. 'But you, you've got it all together. You know where you're going, you've applied for this course, you know what you don't want.' He smiled at her, touched her stomach, sort of elaborating his point and killing her inside at the same time. ‘Well, you don’t want a little one in there, mucking up your future, and I don’t need to be the one who mucks it up.’

‘Hell…’ He pulled his hand away, frowned at the big yellow taxi hooting outside. ‘Don’t go.’

‘I’d better….’ Her head was whirling. She was tempted to tell him and terrified too, terrified of giving him that—*that* other bit of herself that needed to be handed with such tender care. ‘I really do want to see Bernadette.’

‘Come back afterwards? The twins won’t be back till five.’

‘We’ll see.’

And it didn’t end on a row, just a quick but sad kiss, before she climbed into the taxi and headed for home. But not even a shower could clear her head and it wasn’t too many Singapore slings that had her head pounding.

She was scared to trust him.

CHAPTER TWELVE

'WHAT are you doing here?' Bernadette was sitting on the bed with her mum, dressed in real clothes—and looking pretty and terrified as she limped towards the outside world.

'I came to say goodbye!'

'Just for that?' Bernadette said.

'Just for that.' Molly smiled and gave her a cuddle. 'I'm going to miss you.'

'I'm *really* going to miss you!'

And Molly gave her a little friendship ring she'd bought—ten dollars of silver, but worth a fortune.

'Bernadette asked me to get something for you.' Her mum smiled. 'I gave it in at the nurses at the station to pass on. I'll go and get it.'

'You were really sweet to me that night I was crying.' Molly blushed as she recalled it.

'You were nice to me that night too,' Bernadette countered, staring at her ring. 'I really am your friend?'

'Looks like it,' Molly sighed.

'How are things…?' Bernadette asked, and, as good friends did, she trod very carefully. 'I mean, after that night when you were so sad…'

'I'm not sure,' Molly admitted, as she tried to work out in her own mind where she was. 'And I know I sound old and past it, but it really does get more complicated as you get older.'

'Well, if it doesn't work out, I know someone who likes you.' Bernadette gave a shy giggle. 'Dr Luke—he's always watching you when you don't know he is, and he always smiles more when you're working!'

'Here…'

Bernadette took the little bag from her mum. 'You won't believe what it is!'

It was the same ring—well, almost. A little

knot of silver that meant the world, and Molly's eyes filled up when she put it on.

'We're having a little party in a couple of weeks…' Bernadette's mum sort of nodded in the direction of Nathan's bed, saying without words that when Nathan got out it would happen. 'Just a few sausages on the barbecue. I'm sure you'll be busy with work…'

'I'd love to come.' Molly grinned, because she would—really—love to go, and Bernadette would love to have her there—just that little bit of help as she made her transition out of the hospital world and back into the real one.

Transition…

There was that word again, Molly thought as she checked her pigeonhole for her pay slip. She felt her heart skip when she saw the thick white envelope—she hadn't expected to hear till after her days off, had tried to push it out of her mind till then, only here it was.

And she read the letter with mixed feelings, proud of herself but saying goodbye to a bit of her past as she looked to a very busy future—seven a.m. starts mixed with ten p.m. finishes for her practicals, days at school and evenings spent studying.

'Oh, no, not nights.' She heard the moan from Hannah, a grad nurse, as she read the new roster at the nurses' station.

Night duty *did* consume you.

Forced you into an altered existence where you slept during the day and tried to ignore the doorbell and next-door's dog barking and the lawnmower and the phone. Where you sort of learnt how to function in a permanent state of exhaustion—at least, that was how it was for Molly.

But she loved night duty.

Loved the comradeship, the chance to use her brain—because there were few others to pick at night.

They were also great, as Anne Marie and Debbie and so many others had told her, for mothers.

Home in time to take the kids to school.

Up—just—in time to pick them up, get

homework done, give them a bath and dinner and hopefully get them to bed before you turned up yawning for handover.

Or so she'd been told—not that she'd ever expected to find out.

Stuffing the envelope into her bag, Molly knew she wasn't going back to Luke's.

Knew that these five days were for her and her alone.

Turning on her mobile as she headed to the car, she saw two missed calls from him, but her resolve didn't waver.

She indicated left for her house, rather than right for his.

She didn't need to make excuses—that was the bliss of being a transition girl.

There was no one to please except herself—and if she needed some time to think then she'd take it.

'Molly!'

Pressing the hands-free key, Molly waited for a gap in the traffic.

'Hi, Luke.'

'I wasn't sure if you were coming back.'

'Actually, no, Luke—' she started, but he didn't wait for her to finish.

'That's fine. I didn't want you to come home to an empty house. OK, I'll give you a ring tomorrow.'

She could hear the edge in his voice despite the light chatter, could hear the car hooting behind her as she missed her gap in the traffic.

'Is everything all right, Luke?'

'Fine.'

'Luke?' The driver behind her was resting his hand on his horn and Molly waved to him in a rather unladylike fashion.

'Mum just collapsed—I'm on my way to pick up the twins.'

'You didn't need to come,' Luke said when he opened the door that evening.

As she'd driven over, Molly had told herself the same thing—she didn't need to go.

She wanted to.

Wanted to see that he was OK.

Wanted to make his horrible day just a little bit easier.

'But I'm glad you did,' Luke added as he gestured her inside. 'What's that?'

'Take-away noodles,' Molly said, glad that she'd come. 'I don't do casseroles.'

She popped her head into the living room and for once the place wasn't chaotic. There were just two glum, pale faces staring at the television and again ignoring her when she said hello.

'Don't take it personally.' He spoke as she followed him to the kitchen. 'They've had a bad day.'

'Your mother's not too bad?' Molly checked, or at least that was the indication she'd got when he'd briefly called her.

'She fainted.' Luke served up the noodles as he spoke. 'Unfortunately Angus saw it, and panicked, and my aunt's not made of as stern stuff as her sister. Well, she called an ambulance and it sounded like it was chaos for a bit. But it's sorted now—sort of,' he added as he sat down with dinner.

'Sort of?'

'She needs a hysterectomy. She should have had one this month. I assumed it was because of the waiting list and was about to either pull a few strings or, if that didn't work, rip into someone. Only it turns out she's been putting it off till the twins go to school—which is in three months' time.'

'Oh, Luke.'

'I've got her booked in for next Friday.' He gave a tired smile.

'And where does that leave you?' Molly blinked, because from where she was sitting it was hopeless, but Luke had a plan.

Sort of.

'They're going to have to go to day care—full time. Look, I've got my interview on Thursday, and if I get this job, I've already decided that I don't want to land it all on Mum anyway. I knew they'd have to go to day care, even if for just a couple of days a week to give her a break—the start of the school year's just too far off.'

'And if you don't get this job?'

'Day care again!' Luke gave a wry grin. 'I can't do nights—it's just too hard on the twins and too hard on Mum. If I can't pick up enough locum day shifts at the hospital then there's a GP clinic down the road—they're always looking for someone.'

'You don't want to work at the GP clinic, though.'

'It honestly doesn't matter.' Luke gave such a tired smile she knew that tonight it actually didn't. 'I'm going to look at day-care centres this week. I think some of them even have transport that takes the children to kinder so they can still see the little friends they've made. I just hope to God I get this job.' He stood up and went to the fridge. 'Do you want a beer?' He laughed at her screwed up nose. 'Oh, yeah, you hate beer. Wine, then?'

'I'm driving.' She was frowning at his back as he rummaged in the drawer for a bottle opener. 'Well, it's not going to look too good if you take the next few nights off sick before your interview.'

'You sound like my mum. She wants them to sleep there but, Molly, they're shocking even in their own beds.' It was the first time she'd heard him describe them as anything other than perfect little angels. 'Mum's just not well enough, especially before surgery. I'm just going to have to tell Doug what's happened—and if he doesn't get it…'

'I can stay.' She sort of blurted out the words, knowing that if she thought about it too much she'd change her mind, but Luke tried to do it for her.

'No!' He shook his head. 'Molly, a few dinners so you could help with school runs was the deal. Look, it's nearly all sorted.'

'It will be sorted a lot quicker if you get this job,' Molly said, 'and you've got a lot more chance of getting this job if you don't go off sick for the three nights before the interview. It's three nights, Luke. I'm off anyway till Thursday.'

'You must have had plans.'

'Not now. Come on, Luke, I'm not moving in for ever…' Her eyes urgent suddenly, she leant over the table and spoke in a harsh whisper. 'But I'm not sleeping with you!'

'I'm not sleeping with you either!' Luke whispered harshly back, but he was smiling. 'I'm not going to be there at night, remember, so you can have my bed.'

'No.' Molly shook her head. 'It's too weird for the twins. I'll have the sofa.'

'We'll sort something out.' He pushed his noodles away untouched. 'Are you sure about this, Molly?'

'No!' She answered honestly, the metal ring in her brown leather bag that still contained the envelope digging into her as she leant back in her chair and realised that maybe it wasn't space she needed from Luke or the twins to really make up her mind.

It was time.

Time with them.

'Well, she's not sleeping in my bed!' Amelia stamped her foot.

'And she's not sleeping in mine.' Angus folded his arms.

Feeling like Goldilocks in reverse, Molly looked over at Daddy Bear and wished to hell he could say that, actually, no, she was sleeping in his!'

Of course he couldn't.

They'd decided that to get the twins used to the idea she'd stay on Sunday, so while he told them Molly went home and packed a bag, fed the cat and promised him she'd be home while the twins were at kinder. She arrived back at Luke's to find the mother of all tantrums taking place.

'Fine.' Luke shrugged and walked out of the living room and to the hall. 'I'll ring Nanny and say you can stay at hers then.'

'But Nanny's not well!' Angus's eyes were as

wide as saucers, and Amelia nudged him quiet, only it didn't work. 'She might be ill again!'

'Then you'd better be good for her,' Luke answered sternly, 'and go straight to bed when she tells you.' He picked up the phone and turned to Molly. 'Look, thanks, Molly, for offering to help out, but it looks like we won't be needing you after all. I'll ring Mum and let her know.'

As Luke punched in the numbers, Molly picked up her suitcase.

'He isn't really ringing.' Amelia glowered.

Luke flicked it on to speakerphone and there was no mistaking Mrs Williams's voice.

'Harriet Williams speaking!'

'She can sleep in mine,' Angus snarled, then without another word he and Amelia huffed into the living room.

'Glass of wine?' Luke suggested after he'd asked his mother how she was.

'Yes, please.'

Putting down her suitcase, she wandered into the kitchen and put her brown bag back over the chair then took a grateful sip of her wine as she thought about the white envelope sitting in there.

Two minutes into this parenting lark and she wanted to click on her pen.

CHAPTER THIRTEEN

'MORNING, guys!' Molly pushed open the bedroom door and couldn't help but smile. Amelia, in her pyjamas and wings, looked like a fallen angel crashed out on her stomach and her arms and legs like a starfish. Angus peeked out of the sheets and blinked as she turned on the light. 'Time to get up and get ready for kinder. Daddy should be home soon.'

'Morning, Molly.' Angus forgot he wasn't talking to her for two seconds, but when Amelia sat up and gave him a frown, he soon remembered. The little duo pulled on their slippers and shuffled out as Molly padded behind.

'It's the last morning, isn't it?' Amelia checked,

peering over her orange juice. 'Daddy's on nights off now.'

'That's right.'

'What happens next week?' Angus asked, and for once Amelia didn't come up with a quick answer. 'Nanny's having her operation tomorrow,' Angus said as it dawned on him, 'so who's going to look after us?'

And for the first time Amelia looked to Molly for an answer—but that was for Luke to tell them. It certainly wasn't for Molly to somehow explain that their little worlds were about to change yet again, so instead she gave them both a smile.

'Daddy will sort all that out.'

The time with the twins had been well spent because, Molly realised, despite her best efforts, it didn't get easier.

Actually, it did for Luke. He was thrilled that they seemed to be sleeping through. It just didn't get easier for Molly.

Funny, that. She scowled into her coffee as he did Amelia's hair before school.

Not that they'd been naughty—in the three nights she'd had them Luke had put them to bed before he'd left and woken them all up when he'd come home. He was about to take them to kinder.

It was the little barbs when they were awake that Molly was finding it harder and harder to ignore.

'There you go!' Luke had tied her hair into a high ponytail—very well actually—and added a couple of butterfly hairclips. 'Ready for kinder.'

'I need my wings!'

'So you do…' He put them on her. 'Now you're beautiful.'

'Not the *most* beautiful, though. You said that was Mummy!' Just for a second her eyes met Molly's in the mirror. 'Didn't you, Daddy? Didn't you say that Mummy was the most beautiful woman in the world?'

At least he had the grace to look awkward as the twins scampered off to collect their bags.

'What could I say?' He gave a thin smile.

'Nothing.' Molly swallowed. 'But she was rude to me at dinner last night when she said I wasn't good at telling stories—and you didn't say anything then either.'

'I don't think she was being rude,' Luke answered carefully. 'She was just—'

'Comparing me to her mother,' Molly said tightly, then regretted it, felt stupid and petty. Of course the little girl made comparisons, of course she was suspicious and wary, but did she have to be so spiteful—and could Luke really not see it?

'They really didn't wake up in the whole three nights that you had them!' Luke still couldn't believe it. 'And they've been going to bed well too—you've no idea what a difference that is. That's three days, no, four now that there hasn't been a wet bed or a nightmare.'

'Thank goodness for that!' Molly actually managed a genuine smile, then grimaced. 'I hope I just didn't not hear them and sleep right through.'

'Oh, I assure you you'd hear. They must feel really comfortable with you.'

Molly's raised eyebrows didn't go unnoticed, but before she could give a smart response a rather more sensible one came to mind. 'When your mum has them, do they stay there or here?'

'Here,' Luke said. 'We're trying to give them some sort of a routine.'

'And they were good at your aunt's?'

'Golden apparently.'

'Did they sleep in the same room there?'

'They've been sleeping apart since they were three.' Luke shook his head, the solution surely not that simple.

'They hadn't lost their mum then.'

'But they've never even asked to share.'

'Maybe they just need to,' Molly said simply.

The terrible two were back now, pulling on their shoes and talking at the tops of their voices.

'I'll take them to kinder.' He bent over to kiss her, then remembered and pulled back. 'I'll see you in half an hour.'

'I've got to go home this morning.' She saw the question in his eyes, but chose not to answer it. 'You've got to get ready for your interview and I've got some forms I need to fill out.'

'For your course?'

'Yep—they have to be in tomorrow. I'll pick them up, though. What time does your interview finish?'

'I should be back just after one.'

'Well, good luck.' Amelia was calling at the door now as Angus suddenly remembered he hadn't brushed his teeth. 'You're going to get it!'

'I'm not so sure,' Luke admitted. 'I've been out of paeds for so long. I've kept up to date, though. I did do some regular stints in Sydney.'

'Why did you give it up?' Molly frowned. 'I mean, GP's hours are lousy…'

'I could pick and choose at the clinic.'

'But you loved paeds?' Molly pushed. 'Did Amanda work?' She bit her lip, wondering if she'd asked too much, but Luke didn't seem to mind.

'She gave up when she was pregnant. It was a

difficult pregnancy and she never went back. It's hard doing everything with little ones.'

'Daddy!' the twins chorused.

'Thanks again for all this!'

'Really, it's fine.'

And it might have been.

If the twins had given an inch.

There was another very good reason, Molly had started to realise, for keeping little children away from grown-up games: they ruined them!

Despite her best efforts, despite making no effort at all, in the hope it would work, in the weeks since she'd met them, the only thing that had flourished had been an obvious dislike—for *her*.

The cat was delighted to see her, though, mewing at her legs as Molly made a coffee and sat down with her forms.

Go for it!

Luke had been thrilled when she'd told him, had been genuinely pleased for her, she knew that—*knew* that—only she'd seen a flash of something she couldn't quite interpret in his eyes. Regret, disappointment…

And she didn't blame him.

Because she felt them both too.

Oh, he didn't expect her to give up her goals so he could focus on his.

Didn't expect her to put her dreams on hold so she could make his life easier.

In a perfect world no one would have to give up a single thing for it all to work. Couples juggled careers and kids, there were these superwomen who breastfed their way through their PhDs and managed to fit in the gym.

Just Molly wasn't one of them.

And she wasn't a very good transition girl either—because good transition girls didn't go falling in love and thinking about juggling kids and work and whether they might make it—before he'd even asked. Didn't sit there crying when a career break opened up. No, they embraced it with open arms.

Which meant the transition period was over.

Tears in her eyes, Molly picked up her pen.

They'd served their purpose. She'd helped him through a horrible rough patch, massaged his ego and given him a few long-overdue smiles—and he in turn had massaged hers too. She'd started with the sexual confidence of a gnat and was feeling a whole lot better in that department. She had stood up to Richard and moved on from the past.

And it was time to move on from Luke too—because otherwise they were going to settle down and no matter how much she loved him, Molly loved herself more and she'd promised never to settle for second best.

Signing the form, Molly knew she'd made the right choice.

Because second best, to Luke, was what she was.

'Oh, it's you!' Amelia didn't even try to hide the disappointment on her face as kinder spilled out and Molly stood with the real mums, waiting. 'How long will Dad be?'

'He'll probably be home by the time we get

there.' Molly had to unclench her teeth before answering, helping Angus with his laces as Amelia pulled on her ballet pumps.

Amelia was as rude as she could be, and Angus was doing his bit too.

But all that she could have dealt with, Molly thought sadly as they walked to the car.

Four-year-olds with forked tongues Molly could handle.

As long as Luke could see it too.

She'd tried to tell him—gently at first—and now it seemed it was all she did. Moaned about something they'd said, or sat with pursed lips when he appeared not to notice.

Each thinly veiled insult, each little trick was somehow deemed not important when she regaled it to Luke.

'They're kids, Molly,' he'd say with a laugh, trying to make her see the joke, trying to get her to look at the lighter side.

And often she could.

Only this afternoon she couldn't.

'Why's he having an interview when he's already got a job?' Angus actually spoke as she strapped him into his car seat. 'Is he going to be doing a different job?'

'He's at a meeting, silly!' Amelia made sure she strapped herself in.

'No.' Angus was adamant. 'I heard him speaking to Nanny and he said he had an interview.'

'What's an interview?' Amelia frowned.

'To get a different job!'

'He'll still be a doctor,' Molly said, 'and at the same hospital.'

'So why?'

'Daddy's got a very important job,' Molly answered carefully, 'and sometimes you have to be interviewed—it happens all the time. And Amelia's right too.' Her smile at the little girl wasn't returned. 'Today it's more like a meeting.'

She tried chatting as they drove home, but was ignored. Giving in, she turned up the radio as four little blue eyes in the back seat burnt holes in the back of her head.

The trouble with the twins was that that's what they were—trouble.

Molly's rear windows didn't go up and down any more thanks to their frantic pushing, the owner at her local milk bar was struggling even to talk to her since they'd swiped some treats, and her already fragile ego was being dented further from Amelia's constant jibes.

'How old are you, Molly?' Amelia asked sweetly.

'Twenty-nine,' Molly answered, forgetting herself and smiling into the rear-view mirror as Amelia actually talked to her.

'And you *still* don't have a husband!'

'Why are we stopping?' Angus asked at they pulled into the milk bar. 'Are we getting a treat?'

'Not today,' Molly said through gritted teeth. 'I need to post a letter.' Tears stung her eyes as she did just that, because now she had to tell Luke.

Not about the letter, though. About them.

'Here we are,' Molly said, opening up the house, utterly exhausted and longing for a couple of hours in bed before her shift. And even though she wasn't particularly sure if she was going to say it yet, and even if she wasn't particularly looking forward to saying it, still she was awash with relief when Luke's car crunched into the drive. 'And here's Daddy!'

Bearing gifts, too!

'How did it go?' Molly was dying to hear.

'Tell you later! I got some pies for us.' He kissed the twins then headed to the kitchen. 'And some doughnuts for you two, if you eat your lunch!'

'We're not hungry,' Amelia answered. 'It was International Food Day today at kinder, remember!'

'How could I forget?' Luke gave a wry smile at the chaos littering the kitchen benches. 'They told me at bedtime last night.'

'What did you take for International Food Day?' Molly asked.

'Do you want to borrow my lipstick?' Amelia ignored the question with one of her own. 'To make you look prettier?'

'Molly doesn't need lipstick.' Luke laughed, but Molly's face was growing redder.

'I think she does.'

And it was the last straw.

It was the straw that broke the camel's back—or however the saying went. But whatever it was, and whether it was exhaustion or something else, something in Molly snapped as Luke appeared not to notice and just served up the pies.

'Are you going to let her get away with that?' The twins had dashed outside, slamming the door and running down the garden, leaving Molly and Luke sitting in uncomfortable silence—well, uncomfortable for Molly. Luke was just tucking into his pie and then frowning at the tone of her voice.

'With what?'

'Amelia—offering me her lipstick.'

'She was being nice!'

'No, Luke.' Molly shook her head. 'Believe me, she wasn't being nice.'

He rubbed the bridge of his nose with his thumb

and finger, worked his way up to tell her. Only if he did start, he didn't think he'd be able to stop.

And he knew she didn't want to hear it.

Hear about the nightmares and wet beds and the tears and screams that usually filled their nights.

About the notes from kinder and the child psychologist who told him to be patient and just give it time.

That kids dealt with things differently, that kids grieved in different ways, and he should try to keep things normal.

Normal!

'I got the job!' he said instead, totally off subject, but not to him.

'Congratulations!'

'Yeah!'

His head was pounding with neuralgia—he'd got this job and again everything was going to change.

And tonight he had to sit them down and tell them that.

That they were starting in another new place,

that they'd be seeing less of him, and even though in the long run it would be better, the whole thing was changing again.

And now she wanted him to tell off two little kids who were just starting to get it that their mother wasn't coming back.

Not ever.

'They miss their mum,' he said instead, trying to keep his voice even. 'Things are a bit tough right now.'

'I understand that,' Molly said through gritted teeth—only she didn't, or couldn't, or wouldn't.

'And, as careful as we've been, they're not stupid. I think they're starting to work out that we're a bit more than friends—which we are.'

'I'll back off,' Molly said.

'I don't want you to.' And the shift she'd felt was happening again, toppling them both in a dangerous direction. 'You know I want more!'

'I can't.'

'So, what do you want, Molly?' Luke asked. 'You want to keep things casual, you don't want to get too involved, but then you have the temerity to tell me how to raise my kids.'

'I'm not telling you how to raise them.' Molly struggled to keep the rising note out of her voice, because he was right—everything he said was right—but somehow something had to be said. 'Just if every now and then you could defend me…'

'Defend you?' He gave an incredulous snort. 'From four-year-olds?'

'Who can be very rude!' There was a horrible silence, a horrible moment as she said more than she'd meant to, but the genie was out of the bottle now and there was no going back. 'Look, Luke, they need consistency—to know their boundaries…'

'I don't need your opinion on my children, thanks, Molly, when you've made it very clear you don't want to be in their lives…'

'What I'm trying to say…' She ran a tongue over her lips, tried, tried and tried again to put things better, knew she'd handled this appallingly.

'I'm good with children—usually I'm really good with children—but here, in your home…'

'You're good with children at *work*, Molly,' he snapped. 'When you're at work, yes, you're great with kids. But as you've said on several occasions, the mummy thing just isn't for you—and maybe you were wise to make that choice because frankly…'

And she stood there as he killed her with words, as he voiced her deepest, darkest thoughts that maybe there *was* a reason she couldn't have children, maybe she actually *wasn't* good enough to be a mother.

'Their mother died six months ago, for God's sake, and you're upset because Amelia talks about her too much. You want me to defend you—defend *you* who wants nothing more than a *good time*!'

And there was no point.

Just no point in answering back at all.

It was as if they were standing on opposite rocks, screaming over some vast abyss that was just too big and too deep and too impossible to bridge.

And maybe he was right, Molly thought. Maybe she was being unreasonable. And maybe she was right, too, in expecting a little bit of back-up from him every now and then. Only that wasn't the point either.

'It's not about the kids,' Molly croaked. 'It's about you and what you did. You left me for her, you sat in that café and told me that you missed her more than you'd expected to, that what we'd had…' And it was as brutal to repeat the words as it had been to hear them. 'Just didn't measure up to what you had going with Amanda. And, you know, every time I walk in this place I'm reminded of that fact—that I'm not as good, that I'm not as funny or as beautiful or as clever.'

'Molly…don't.'

'I wasn't good enough. You made that clear. And now that she's gone, suddenly I am. How do you think that makes me feel, Luke?' And she could see it now, could almost hear what Anne Marie had been about to say, could actually articulate the hurt that been eating away since the second he'd walked back into her life. 'How do you think it makes me feel when on numerous occasions I'm reminded of that fact?'

'It's not like that.'

'But it is. This house is like a shrine to Amanda—and you wonder why I feel uncomfortable. I'll tell you why—because not for a minute am I allowed to forget that I'm second best.'

'Molly—'

Only she wasn't listening. Tears streamed down her face as it all came out. 'Oh, I'm good enough to have a laugh with, good enough to sleep with, good enough to drop the kids at kinder or pick them up if you're busy. You're probably quite fond of me, given I'm so nice. Hey, if things had kept going on I might have even made it as the next Mrs Williams—only I wasn't the first! And it had nothing to do with timing and everything to do with that you didn't want me enough, you wanted her!'

'I told you—she was pregnant.'

'I can never win, then…' Her nose ran in lieu

of tears as he shook his head in confusion. 'I'm never going to win.'

'What are you talking about?'

'This.' Closing her eyes, she seared her heart with impossibility and found the voice to ask the most difficult questions of them all. 'What if *I'd* been pregnant, Luke?' She watched him swallow, watched his jaw clench as she posed the impossible. 'What if that day, when you came to tell me we were over, I'd told you I was pregnant too?'

And the answer was there in his silence, a loaded silence where *nothing* was the worst thing you could hear.

'Thanks.' She spat out the word.

'You don't understand.'

'And I'm not even going to try to.'

'Meaning?'

'Meaning we're finished.'

'Because of something that happened five years ago.'

'Because it's still happening now!' Molly rasped.

'I'm crazy about you, Molly. I want you in my life—more of you, not less.'

'Yes! Now—when you *need* a wife—it looks like I might just fit the bill!'

'You're never going to forgive me for it, are you?'

'No!' Molly shook her head, realised the truth—a little too late, perhaps, but it was here now and she was ready to face it. 'No, Luke, you're right. I'm never going to get past it.'

Amelia and Angus were running down the garden towards the house, curls flying, bouncing a ball, and there was no reason to stay around to say goodbye—she'd be missed as much as she'd been made welcome—so, picking up her keys, Molly headed down the hall. And, childish as it was, she even poked her tongue out at a smiling photo of Amanda as Luke just stood there.

And there was nothing that would have stopped her walking out, nothing she was needed for, except…

Molly wasn't sure what came first, the crack of glass breaking or the piercing sound of a child screaming out. The hall had never seemed longer. The couple of seconds it took her to run was enough time for Amelia to pick herself up, for her scream to subside. And there was a second of stunned silence, just one pause as the child stared down at her arm, her eyes bulging, frantically running with a different sort of scream now, hysterical, frantic screams as her arm pumped blood…

Arterial blood, Molly acknowledged as she dashed forward. Arterial because it was spurting out. With every frantic heartbeat from Amelia she bled, spraying the walls with blood, just flailing and panicking, till Molly grabbed her.

'It's OK.' Molly was shouting over her, holding her little arm high and pressing hard inside her elbow as Luke dashed over. 'Get a teatowel,' Molly shouted. 'Something! It's OK, honey.' Over and over she said the words to Amelia, holding her terrified eyes. 'It's stopping. Daddy's putting something on it.'

Luke pressed the teatowel against the wound

and held it, his face chalk-white, his breathing rapid and shallow as he tried to reassure his daughter, tried to shout over the screams. It took a moment for Molly to register that it wasn't Amelia screaming now but Angus, still standing at the door where Amelia had fallen, his expression one of abject terror.

'She's OK, Angus.'

'It's happening again!' He was running, screaming, chanting. 'It's happening again!'

'Angus, she's OK,' Molly called. 'She's going to be just fine. Daddy's going to call an ambulance.'

'It will be quicker to drive—' Luke started, but Molly spoke more firmly. There was no way they could get in the car, especially with Angus so hysterical.

'Daddy's going to call an ambulance, and we're going to get Amelia to hospital and get her arm fixed.'

Amelia was so brave, just staring at Molly and nodding, her little face white, shocked and terrified. She was close to fainting, leaning into

Molly, who sat on the floor and pulled her onto her knee, still holding up her arm as Luke grabbed the phone.

'Angus, it's OK.' Luke was trying to talk over him, but it was impossible. Angus's petrified wailing just added to the chaos as Luke ran out into the hall to be heard.

'Angus…' Molly said helplessly, trying to calm him down, hearing Luke trying to get the details out to the operator.

'Angus, I'm the one who's hurt!' It was Amelia's indignant wail that halted him, just for a second, and as he opened his mouth to scream, it was Amelia who got there first. 'Tell us a story, Molly.'

Golly!

'Molly's going to tell us a story!' Amelia said. 'Like I did when Mummy wasn't well.'

So Molly did…about a little girl who'd cut herself, and the nice paramedics who would come. She pressed on Amelia's arm, holding it high, as Luke came back. She told her about the ambulance that would take her to hospital as Luke tied another teatowel over the sodden one, then held Angus, who was quiet now but looked stunned, watching bewildered and scared as the paramedics came marching in, efficient and calming.

'You're so brave…' Molly cuddled Amelia closer as a paramedic slipped on an oxygen mask, put in an IV and delivered a swift bolus of saline solution.

'She's getting some special medicine to help with the pain.' Luke's voice was thick from emotion as he sat beside them, stroking Amelia's little face and holding Angus.

Things were calmer now. The bleeding, which had been awful, had been stemmed by a blood-pressure cuff that would be released every few moments. As Amelia was lifted onto the stretcher, Luke rang his mother and the hospital to let them know they were on their way, but one look at the ambulance and Angus started crying again.

'I'll stay here with him,' Molly offered. 'You go. Your mum will be here soon.' But Angus was inconsolable, screeching in terror as they approached the ambulance, his hands grabbing at his dad's neck as Molly tried to take him from Luke.

'Molly can come with me.' Little and brave, and just so much older than her tender years, it was Amelia who took charge. 'You stay with Angus, Daddy, till Nanny gets here. I'll be fine with Molly.'

And the saddest part for Molly was the devastation and helplessness on Luke's usually strong face when he bent and kissed his daughter goodbye, the impossibility of the situation, having to let his sick child go to look after the other. The indecision, where nothing he could do was right.

'Look after her.' He screwed his eyes closed. 'I didn't mean it like that. I know you'll look after her. I'll be five minutes behind…'

'We've got to go,' Molly said as they clipped in the stretcher. 'I'll see you at the hospital. She'll be OK.'

She was!

Despite morphine, despite losing a considerable amount of blood and the horrors of earlier, her suspicious, wary eyes remained open, frowning at everyone who came too close—everyone, that was, except Molly, almost as if they were in this together. Her little chin was set and defiant as they arrived at the hospital and were wheeled straight in. Mark Lawson, the trauma consultant, must have been alerted and was waiting for his colleague's daughter.

'Hello, Emily.' He gave her a smile as he pulled on his gloves.

'Amelia,' Molly said.

'Amelia,' he corrected himself. 'I'm just going to have a very quick look. How long's the cuff been up?'

'Five minutes,' the paramedic answered.

'OK. Once I take the dressing down I want to have a look. Then release it when I say so. Can we have some better light here?' There were people pulling lights, ripping open dressings, changing over the oxygen and IV poles, but even though Molly knew exactly what was going on, even though she'd done the same, or similar, on numerous occasions, today it was just too much. Today all she could see was Amelia, her little fairy wings poking out, staring up at the ceiling and trying not to cry.

'Daddy will be here soon.' Molly squeezed the fingers of Amelia's good hand as she grimaced in pain. 'You're doing really well.'

'Where is Luke?' Mike frowned. 'I want to get her straight up.'

'Five minutes away,' Molly answered, but she was only half listening.

'Let's prep her for Theatre and get her up as soon as Luke arrives.' Which was quick, but wasn't special treatment. Stemming the bleeding with the blood-pressure cuff wasn't ideal, and Amelia needed the artery repaired as quickly as possible, but the fact it was Mark Lawson giving the order had everyone moving even more rapidly.

'Hi, there, sweetie, I'm Karan. We're just going to get you out of these clothes and pop you into one of our gowns.'

'I can do that,' Molly said, untying Amelia's runners.

'We'll need some nail-polish remover,' Karan called through the curtains.

'You love your make-up, don't you?' Molly grinned, but it faded as Karan came over with scissors.

'We're going to have to cut your wings off, Amelia.' She didn't say no. What was worse was that she just seemed to shrink back into the pillow, her blue eyes blinking rapidly, then closing, only not enough to stop a big tear rolling down into her hair.

'Can the wings stay?' Molly's hand came between the scissors and the elastic because, yes, they had to come off and, yes, with her arm seriously injured and a drip in the other, the only way was to cut them, but she knew the anguish it would cause Amelia. Knew that she'd worn them, slept in them, lived in them since her mother had died.

'We need to get her top off and get her into the gown, and there's the drip on her good arm.'

'Cut off her top,' Molly said, gently brushing back Amelia's hair with her fingers. But her voice and eyes were firm as she addressed Karan. 'The wings stay on.'

And Karan gave her an eye-roll, because clearly the wings *would* have to come off—but they could be cut off once Amelia was under anaesthetic, and then Molly would get a needle and thread from somewhere and sew them up before Amelia woke up.

'They're staying on,' Molly said firmly to Amelia, 'and when you wake up they'll still be on. But we might have to tape them to you for a while—does that sound OK?'

Amelia nodded and stared up at the ceiling, then for the first time turned her eyes on Molly and looked at her without distrust, spoke to her without distaste. 'My mummy bought them for me.'

'I know she did,' Molly said, 'and they're beautiful.'

'My mummy was beautiful, too!'

CHAPTER FOURTEEN

'How's Angus?'

'Mum's with him. She knows how to deal with him—he'll be OK.' Luke had his head in his hands, but every now and then he'd look up at the clock. 'They're taking a while.'

'Microsurgery tends to,' Molly said logically, but she was looking at the clock too. 'Angus was…' She tried to find a word that came close to even describing his reaction. 'Devastated.'

'He'll be fine,' Luke insisted, and she looked over at him, elbows on his knees, biting down on his knuckles, as ill and as grey as a healthy man could look. She knew that his angst wasn't solely reserved for Amelia, knew that when he looked at her next he'd confirm what she was starting to know and hoping to God that she'd say the right thing.

'When you asked what I'd do if I found out you were pregnant… Aside from what I wanted, I guess I knew you'd be OK—with or without me, that you'd do the right thing. But Amanda…'

And finally he was ready to say it—and she was ready to hear it.

'Amanda was ill.' Green eyes awash with pain finally met hers, that talk he'd attempted taking place now, in the stark confines of a hospital waiting room. 'Mentally ill. She wasn't simply run over—she was in full-blown psychosis and she ran straight out into the street, or so I'm told. She'd been missing for a couple of days.' He gave a tight smile that was utterly devoid of humour. 'She went missing quite a lot. Look, I know I'm soft on the twins but, hell, if you knew what they'd been through…'

'You should have told me.'

'She was their mother.' Luke swallowed. 'And

it's something…I didn't want to say it to someone who didn't want to get involved.'

And she could understand that, understand how private that pain was, because she had her own private pain too, that piece inside that had to be divulged carefully.

'I know you don't gossip, Molly. Hell, I'm not asking you not to tell anyone. It's just not something I want everyone knowing—for the twins' sake, more than anything. I tell them in my own way. They see a child psychologist and they're starting to talk about it.' He gave a wry smile. 'Which is all too much information for a transition girl!'

'How long was she ill for?'

'I don't know.' Luke said. 'I think it must have been since medical school, from bits I've worked out. The problem was Amanda refused to accept she was ill, helped along by her parents. I didn't know at first. You met her—she was charming, busy, high-achieving, stunning. She just blew me away. But it soon became obvious there was a problem—well, obvious to me. I called round one evening and I hardly recognised her. The flat was like a bomb had hit it, she wasn't washed, wasn't dressed, she wasn't even speaking. I took her up to Sydney to her parents'. She was insistent that I couldn't walk away from her, saying could we give it another go, that she was just tired, that work had just caught up with her. She'd just finished on the neonatal ward before she came to Melbourne, and I knew she'd found it tough, but I sort of knew it was more than that…' He dragged a hand through his hair. 'She was just so low. Of course I couldn't just end it. Next thing I knew she was back, and for a while there I honestly thought I must have imagined the whole thing—you know, exaggerated it in my mind, because she was as bright and as vibrant as she had always been. I really thought it had just been a bad patch, and then…' She could see the turmoil in his face, the pain, the confusion as he relived it, tried to put the craziness of the past few years into some sort of sensible order. 'You know how busy she always was.' He looked at Molly for confirmation and she nodded. 'Sometimes it was much more than that. I'd find her in the study at three o'clock in the morning. She was going to go to Africa, she'd say, and then she'd decide she was going to go to India. She'd get all the brochures. Or she'd suddenly have this brilliant idea about a treatment…' He shook his head in helplessness. 'It just got crazier and crazier—shopping, ridiculous spending, designer shoes, dresses.'

'This is when you were just going out with her?' Molly checked.

'And when I was married to her,' Luke replied. 'Not all the time, of course—there were pockets of normality. But when it happened the first time I ended it. Not just like that. I took her back to her parents'. Some journey that was. And again they insisted there wasn't a problem. I knew that I couldn't live like that, especially given Amanda was so reluctant to help herself. I came back and all I felt was relief—relief that it was over. I didn't ask you out for a while. I figured if she came back and heard I was with someone else, it would just add fuel to the fire. But when I heard that she'd resigned…'

'Why didn't you tell me?' Molly asked. 'We were so close. Why did you feel you couldn't tell me?'

'She was terrified of losing her job—or rather her parents were, if it ever got out. That's why they tried to keep it quiet. They just refused to accept she had a psychiatric problem—just point-blank refused to accept it. And Amanda listened to them. She listened to them when they said it would affect her career if it got out, listened to all the rubbish they fed her. You know, I hate them more than I ever thought it possible to hate other human beings. Amanda had a treatable condition—sure, there would have been highs and lows, even with medication, but not like the ones we had to go through.'

'That's why you were upset with Carl's mum?'

Luke nodded. 'The same way Carl needed his

medication, Amanda needed hers—and by denying it, by assuming it would go away…well, in the end it killed her.'

'Luke, it was Amanda's fault too. She was a doctor, for goodness' sake.'

'She was ill, Molly.' He halted her. 'She had an illness. When I found out she was pregnant…' He took her hand. Not in a romantic way, more as if he was holding on to stop himself falling apart. Molly could actually envisage it, the fear, the trapped feeling he must surely have had. 'I didn't know what to do. We'd been careful, but I guess careful doesn't always work. If I had told you, what would you have said?'

'I don't know…' Molly's mind raced to the past, to a younger, less wise version of herself, dizzy with love and hope, and tried to imagine what she would have done. 'I'd have tried to help. Even if you'd had to marry her, be with her, you could have had a friend—'

'An out,' Luke interrupted. 'Molly, I was so hard on you that day because it *had* to be completely over between us. I couldn't put you through what I knew I was going to go through. And, God help me, during those first couple of years of marriage, if I'd have known you were on the other end of the phone, if I'd have thought we had anything, *anything* we could have built on, I don't know that I could have stayed.'

'You did, though,' Molly croaked. 'You stayed.'

'She wasn't all bad. There were good times, and when she was good…'

'What about when she wasn't good?' Molly asked, because she didn't want to hear excuses, had seen Angus's reaction today, knew that, however good the good times had been, the bad had been far worse. 'What was it like for the twins?'

'Hell.' His voice was just a raw ball of pain. 'This afternoon must have been like a rerun. Not the blood, just the screaming, the chaos. You try to keep it from them, but—'

'How?' Molly blinked. 'How could you possibly keep it from them when they lived with it?'

'I worked at the clinic, walk-in, walk-out, that

was the only job I could do. I'd work while they were in day care. And I'd take them away sometimes, come down to Melbourne to see Mum. It wasn't all bad…' He shook his head in hopeless regret. 'Sometimes she was great—just the best mum. That's what I try to let them remember.'

'I understand that…I can see that now.' Molly nodded, but her mind was whirring. 'Did you ever think of leaving?' Molly asked. 'You taking the twins and raising—?'

'She was their mum, Molly,' Luke rasped. 'I couldn't take them from her; it would have killed her. She adored them…and there were good times.'

And it was the only bit she didn't get—the only bit she couldn't forgive—sitting sobbing at a restaurant and lugging around a broken heart for a while was nothing, nothing compared to what the twins had endured.

'You know why I left you like that.' Luke's voice seemed to be coming from a long way off, as if he were speaking from behind a wall—his features, his emotions just so not in her picture that she actually had to force herself to listen, to drag her mind from the twins and focus on him. 'I'll talk to Amelia—'

'Amelia and I are fine,' Molly interrupted.

'Can we try again?' Luke asked. 'Now that you know?'

She was saved from answering by the theatre nurse popping her head round the door and telling Luke he could come and see Amelia in the recovery ward.

'Has she got her wings on?' Molly checked.

'They're taped to the back of her gown!' the theatre nurse said. 'She's a bit scared and teary, but that's quite usual when they come out of anaesthetic.'

'Come?' Luke offered, but Molly shook her head.

'I have to go.' And she did, because that was what mums or stepmums or one-day-might-be stepmums did, and that, Molly realised now, was something she never would be.

'Surely—?'

'For five minutes, then,' Molly relented—only not for Luke. She'd taken Amelia to Theatre, it was right that she should stay to see she was OK. 'Then I'd better go and get some sleep before work.'

'Daddy…' Loaded with drugs, Amelia had let her barriers down. Her face was wet with tears, sobs shuddering through her little body. 'Don't leave me.' Her free arm wrapped around his neck, the alarms on her drips all going off as she clung to her father.

'I'm not going anywhere.'

'Stay with me!'

'You know I will.'

'I want Mummy.'

'I know you do, baby.'

Molly had never seen him cry, could never have pictured it, really—he was so strong, so tough, and so, so Luke. Molly didn't know what was more heartbreaking—hearing Amelia's wretched sobs or watching the tears slide down his cheeks as he held his daughter, as he missed his wife.

'I'll go,' Molly said softly. 'I'll see you tonight, Amelia—you've been so brave.'

And she tried not to think about it, operated on complete autopilot, even stopped at the gift shop and bought a teddy for Amelia, just as one would have for a friend's sick child.

A friend.

Friends were all they could ever be. Molly knew that now, and it had nothing to do with her feelings for the twins—

And everything to do with her feelings for Luke.

CHAPTER FIFTEEN

'THANK you.' A *very* polite Amelia took from Molly the teddy she had bought at the gift shop. 'She's lovely!'

'He!' Molly winked. 'The tag on his ear says Bert.'

'Bert the bear!' Luke smiled. 'Thanks.'

'I hear you've done really well.'

'She has!' Luke said proudly—and she had. Molly had been given all the details at handover. Two and a half hours on the table for a radial artery and tendon repair and now she was sitting up in bed, talking. It showed what a tough little thing she was. Her arm had been placed in a back slab so that though her arm was immobilised the wound could still be checked.

She was having hourly vascular obs overnight, but though she'd need some antibiotics and physio, the surgeons were pleased so far and hopeful she'd make a full recovery.

'I have to stay in for two nights, maybe three,' Amelia said importantly, 'so I can have antibiotics.' Her face was pale, but it pinked up just a touch as for the second time in as many minutes she practised her manners.

'Thank you for helping me today.'

'I'm glad I could help.'

'And I'm sorry…' Her little voice trailed off, but Molly helped her out.

'It was an accident!' Molly said gently. 'There's nothing to be sorry for.'

'I meant I'm sorry I've been so mean to you.'

Molly's eyes snapped to Luke—she was annoyed that he'd said anything, especially today—but his wide eyes told her that he was as surprised by Amelia's apology as Molly was.

'It's OK.' Molly smiled.

'I told Angus to be mean to you too—so that you'd go away and leave us alone!'

'Amelia!' Luke was clearly shocked, but Molly still smiled.

'That was a pretty good plan!'

'And I'm sorry we stole from the milk bar!'

'They *stole*!' From the look on Luke's face it was lucky that Amelia *had* just had surgery. 'Why didn't you say anything?'

'Because I sorted it out at the time.' Molly blushed. 'And you were asleep. It really wasn't as bad as it seems.'

'Anything else?'

'The car windows…' Amelia mumbled, even as Molly shook her head to tell her to stop.

'Amelia, just what's been going on?'

'I didn't want you to get a girlfriend and neither did Angus—and we thought if we were really horrible and you didn't like us then you wouldn't like Dad any more.'

'Your dad and I are just friends,' Molly said softly.

'You're not his girlfriend?' Amelia checked, and Molly shook her head. 'Is it because of us?'

'Of course not,' Molly said firmly. 'Your dad and I were friends years ago, before you were even born.'

'Er, Molly…' Embarrassed, uncomfortable, Luke stood up. 'Could I have a quick word?' And it was the most exquisitely difficult conversation, made worse because they were standing in the corridor. 'I don't want to lie to her. I mean, we don't have to say too much but…'

'You don't have to lie to her—we're just friends, Luke.'

'Look, Molly, I know what I said back at the house was harsh. I honestly didn't realise how bad the twins were being—you were right to say something. And, yes, I've been too soft on them.'

'I know why now,' Molly answered, 'and I was being pretty childish too.'

'And you know now about Amanda.'

'I understand all that, Luke.' She ran a worried hand over her forehead, didn't want to tell him how she felt, didn't want to criticise that part of him. 'Look, I'll be around for her a bit. I can help while she's in hospital, and I'll pop around now and then, as friends do.'

'Just friends.' Luke had heard the emphasis in her voice and winced.

'Just friends.' Molly's voice wobbled a touch, but her nod was adamant.

'Because of the twins?'

'Because of the twins.' Molly nodded, and it was the truth, only not in the way Luke thought. 'I'd better get on.'

'You're crazy about him,' Anne Marie muttered, 'and he's crazy about you, and the reason he thinks you're backing off is because you don't want his kids…but you do.'

'Leave it.' Molly glared. They were sitting at the nurses' station, hastily writing up notes as the birds started chirping, trying to summon energy to start the morning round. One day post-op Amelia was with her father, who was dozing in a chair beside her just a few beds away. 'You yourself warned me about him.'

'OK,' Anne Marie said. 'I admit I was worried. You were running his kids around, sleeping with him, helping him out—and I thought maybe he was using you a fraction. Given how he'd dumped you in the past, I thought it was a bit rich that suddenly you were good enough!' Molly closed her eyes as Anne Marie voiced every doubt that had plagued her. 'But you know why now, Molly. You know why he had to leave you like that.'

'He could have left her.'

'It's not that straightforward.'

'He could have left if it was so bad.'

'You don't know what that guy had to go through!'

'I know a bit of what the kids went through, though,' Molly snapped, and even though she felt disloyal to Luke, to her best friend it had to be said. 'And I've seen firsthand the effect it had on them. And he stayed—stayed waiting for the good Amanda to come back.'

'It's never that easy. She was ill—he had loyalty to her too. She was the mother of his children.'

'Not when over and over she refused to face her problem, refused to get help, refused to take her meds…'

'Because she was *ill*!' Anne Marie snarled. 'You're making out it was a black-and-white choice. Living with mental illness must be hell. He was doing his best.'

Molly shook her head and stood up, picking up the kidney dish which contained Amelia's IV meds. 'His best for Amanda,' Molly said, 'when his first loyalty should have been to his kids. He should never have exposed them to that. So, just leave it, Anne Marie.'

'How are you feeling?' Molly whispered, and smiled as Amelia's eyes peeked open.

'Itchy! And I need to go to the loo,' she grumbled.

Molly frowned, immediately stopping the medication she was giving, worried she was having a reaction. 'Itchy—where—?'

'My wings,' Amelia moaned. 'They're digging in my back.' They were, and Molly fiddled with them for a moment as Luke stirred on the chair. 'Maybe I could take them off,' Amelia said. 'Have them on the bed beside me.'

'That's a great idea, but they might get lost with the linen. I know…' Molly smiled at Luke as he caught up with the conversation. 'Why don't we tape them to the top of your bed? Then you can see them. And why don't you grab a coffee?' she added as Luke, as stiff as a board, stood up and stretched. 'I'll be awhile.'

Amelia's arm was suspended in a sling attached to an IV pole, her fingers checked regularly for colour, warmth and sensation, and her other hand was attached to an IV. Frankly, it would have been far easier to give her a bedpan, but it was time for her to be up and walking and, anyway, Amelia hated the things, so locating slippers and letting down her arm and putting it in a sling, then shuffling off to the loo was the order of the day. And while they were there it made sense to take her wash bag and freshen her up a bit.

'I can't brush my teeth.' Amelia scowled. 'My arm's in a sling.'

'You've got one good hand,' Molly pointed out.

'I've got a drip in that arm. And I've got a wobbly tooth!'

'Then you'd better clean it properly because the tooth fairy doesn't leave much for dirty teeth!' Molly said sweetly, squeezing some toothpaste onto the brush. 'And I'll do your hair *while* you brush your teeth.' Amelia's beautiful blue eyes narrowed into slits as she eyed Molly's reflection in the mirror, but Molly ignored them, smiling brightly and chatting away as she ran a brush through Amelia's knotted hair. 'The drip should come down once you've had your breakfast, though they'll keep the little plug so that you can have some more medicine.'

'When can I go home?'

'Tomorrow, probably,' Molly answered,

'though you're going to be bandaged up and wearing a sling for a while.'

'I want to go home today.'

'I know,' Molly said, still brushing her hair. Dealing with children who wanted to go home was a normal, everyday part of her job. 'And you will be going very soon, but you really need to be here for another night or so, just so we can make sure your arm's healing nicely. It was a big operation.'

'Angus will be worried—he doesn't like it when things change.' Dealing with children who wanted to go home to look after their siblings wasn't quite so run of the mill. 'And I gave him a big fright yesterday.'

'I bet you got one, too.' Molly tied Amelia's hair into a loose ponytail and stopped talking to Amelia's reflection in the mirror, talking to the top of her blonde head instead as she stared down at the sink.

'It was good that you were there,' came her little voice. 'When Mum wasn't well, I used to tell Angus a story.' Molly continued to fiddle with her hair, brushed the little knotty ends and then retied the bows on the back of her gown. 'She was ill quite a lot.'

'That must have been hard for you.'

'I guess.' Amelia shrugged. 'She was funny too, though, and sometimes she was just like Mum. She was really pretty.'

'I know she was,' Molly agreed. 'I met her when she worked here.'

'Did you like her?'

'I didn't know her that well.' Molly gave a smile. 'To tell you the truth, I was a bit jealous of her. She was really clever and, yes, you're right—she was very pretty.' She was telling the truth and it felt easy—oh, not the truth, the whole truth and nothing but the truth, but from the way Amelia's eyes lit up it was everything she needed to hear. 'Tell you what, I'll speak to your dad, and once you've had breakfast I'll see if we can sort it so that Angus can come in and visit you. He'll feel better when he can see for himself that you're OK.'

Climbing back into her bed, washed, brushed and freshened up, Amelia surveyed the ward as if she were the queen on her throne, wrinkling up her nose at the apple juice Debbie brought her. 'I prefer orange juice!'

Then she spat it out when she got her request.

'Ugh, it tastes disgusting.'

'Because you've just brushed your teeth.' Molly grinned as Anne Marie rolled her eyes.

'Little madam,' Anne Marie muttered once they were safely out of earshot. Normally Molly would have laughed, or agreed, or rolled her eyes, only she didn't. The strangest feeling was bubbling inside her, an angry retort on the tip of her tongue, which she quickly bit back. 'You can tell her daddy's a doctor!'

'She's four and she's scared!' This time Molly didn't hold back, but Anne Marie just grinned.

'Listen to you.' Anne Marie laughed. 'Making excuses— just like an over-protective mother!' She stopped her teasing as Luke came over.

'I was just speaking to Amelia.' Molly gestured

him out of the ward. 'She's really worried about Angus. I said that I'd talk to you, that maybe we could arrange to bring him in this morning.'

'Mum's having surgery.' Luke shook his head. 'Her sister's staying with Angus for now and she doesn't drive.'

'Oh…well, I could bring him.' Molly blushed as she offered and blushed a bit more as Luke shook his head.

'We'll be fine.'

'She really is worried about him.'

'Then I'll get her to ring him.'

'Fine…' Molly cleared her throat. 'If you need a hand next week…'

'We'll be fine.'

'Luke—'

'Molly don't.' He glared at her.

'I'm just trying to help.'

'Well, I don't need your help. I told you, I got the job.'

'Congratulations!' she said again. Only she wasn't smiling. Tears were filling her eyes as the inevitable happened, as Luke took away the one thing they'd promised to keep.

'I start in a couple of weeks, and they've agreed I can take time off till then. So we'll manage fine.'

'I thought—'

'We'd be friends?' Luke finished for her. 'Well, so did I. It just didn't work out that way, I guess.'

'Luke, please.'

'Please, what?' Luke snapped. 'I can't play your game, Molly. I can't just take the bits you're prepared to give and to hell with the rest. You don't want my kids—you've made it clear from the start—and I'm sorry if it's a bit late for me to realise that, but you know what? I actually find that quite offensive! So, no, I don't want you driving the kids around and helping us out when clearly it's the last thing you want to do. And, no, I don't particularly want to be friends right now—let's just see if we can manage civil.'

CHAPTER SIXTEEN

'HERE.' Looking more than a touch awkward, and attempting to be civil, Luke deposited a box of luxury gourmet chocolate biscuits at the nurses' station. 'Seeing how you've fed me the last couple of nights…'

As an IV blared out its alarm, both Anne Marie and Molly jumped to their feet, practically racing to get it—Anne Marie hoping to leave Luke and Molly alone, and Molly hoping to avoid just that.

'Talk to her,' Anne Marie said, pushing a mug of coffee over to him.

'It's a bit hard when she can't stand to be in the same room as me.' Luke gave an exasperated shrug. 'Anyway, there's no point.'

'No point at all,' Anne Marie agreed, with more than a dash of irony.

'We want different things,' Luke snapped. 'Look, I don't want to discuss it.'

'Then don't.' Anne Marie shrugged.

'She doesn't want to get involved…' Luke tore the wrapping off the biscuits '…which is fine. Once we get past this bit, we'll go back to being friends.'

'Given how the sex-buddy thing didn't work out too well?' Anne Marie gave him a tight smile.

'That was her idea!' Luke's face actually reddened a touch. 'She doesn't want kids, and I happen to come with two—so, no, it's never going to work in the long term. Have a biscuit.'

Anne Marie's hand reached out for one, then suddenly pulled back.

'I don't want one.'

'Yes, you do.' Luke frowned, because Anne Marie always did!

'I really don't,' Anne Marie insisted.

'Belgian chocolate,' Luke teased. 'And macadamia nuts.'

'I can't have one.' Anne Marie's face was bright red.

'Can't?'

'I'm on a diet.'

'Oh, sorry.' Luke pulled the biscuits back over to him. 'You should have just said.'

'Well, you don't always want everyone knowing your business.' Anne Marie gulped, her face practically purple now. 'There's a big difference between don't and can't. Sometimes it's just easier to say you don't want something. I mean…' Her eyes were urgent as she met his frown. 'I don't want you knowing all about my cellulite, now, do I?'

'I guess not.'

'So it's easier just to…' Her voice trailed off as Molly returned. 'I'm going to do a check.'

'I've just done one!' Molly said.

'Well, I'm doing another one.'

'What's up with her?' Molly frowned.

'Sick of us two, probably.'

'Probably…' Molly gave a watery smile then looked away.

'I came on too strong yesterday.'

'It doesn't matter.' Molly tried to focus on her notes.

'But it does. You were wonderful with Amelia. If you hadn't been there, I shudder to think what might have happened.'

'Well, she's fine now,' Molly said without looking up, trying to write her notes as she felt him watching her.

And he watched.

Saw for the first time how the years had changed her.

Saw the hard shell she'd wrapped around the softest of hearts—because she'd had to, Luke realised with utter regret.

'I can never win, then.'

He recalled her words and understood them—understood now about transition guys and holding back and never letting him get close so he couldn't break her heart…

Again.

'Can you feed Joseph!' A harassed-looking Hannah dumped the baby and bottle on her boss. 'I've got Louise screaming.'

'Sure,' Molly said, somehow holding the baby and bottle with one hand and still managing to write her notes with the other. Sort of bobbing him on her knee and chatting as she wrote, multi-tasking as women could.

She wanted babies. Luke knew it for certain now. But she didn't want his—which meant, Luke finally realised, that she didn't want him.

'Friends are honest, Mol.' It was Luke who broke the tenuous silence, watched as she looked up and swallowed. 'It isn't about the twins, is it?'

'I don't know what you mean.'

'Us. It's not because of the twins that we didn't make it.'

'I don't want kids, Luke.' She flushed under his scrutiny. 'The stepmum thing just isn't—'

'Molly, please.'

'OK—I don't want to raise the kids of the woman you left me for.'

'But you know why now.'

He was inviting pain. Molly could feel her eyes well with tears as he pushed her to say what she didn't want to.

'It's not about the twins, is it?'

'No…' She shook her head, a great big tear moving too fast for her hand as she attempted to drop her pen and catch it. 'Well, not in that way…'

'What way, then?'

'You stayed.' Two bleak words that somehow filled a forest, two little words that somehow got straight to the horrible point.

'There was no other way.'

'You should have found a way, Luke.'

And it was as simple and as complicated as that. She could understand now, forgive him, even, for leaving her as he had, but the fact that he'd stayed, all that the twins had endured, was something Molly couldn't get past.

It was as if every minute of the last five years had

caught up with him, his face a map of weariness, regret and pain. 'I'm going to lie down.' His voice was strained, his face as white as the sheets on the linen trolley, his back taut with tension as he turned and walked away—then changed his mind. 'Who the hell made you God and judge, Molly?'

It was the longest night.

Knowing, knowing they wouldn't even come out of this as friends—that with the honesty he'd demanded they'd killed whatever they'd somehow salvaged.

Anne Marie's usual happy-go-lucky demeanour was horribly absent as they stood in the drug room and checked the morning's IVs.

'You think he's right—don't you?' Molly's voice was strained.

'I think he has a point.' Anne Marie didn't look up, the vials of antibiotics getting the most thorough of checks. 'And, yes, I think you have one too.'

'It couldn't have worked—'

'No,' Anne Marie broke in, speaking the truth

Molly had hoped she'd never hear. 'It could never have worked out between you two—not if you don't respect him as a parent. Oh, you wouldn't…' Anne Marie flicked bubbles out of a syringe and clamped her lips together.

'Say what you were going to.'

'No.'

'Please…' Molly's face was pale, her lips taut as she confronted her friend. 'You were going to say I wouldn't understand.'

'It's hard, being a parent.' Anne Marie was still tapping the syringe, not that there were any bubbles. 'And sometimes you get it wrong, sometimes you make mistakes, sometimes little things and sometimes big. And when you do, you have to learn somehow to forgive yourself for not being a perfect parent.'

'And that's something I couldn't possibly understand, I suppose?' Molly snapped sarcastically. 'Because I'm not one.' And she waited for Anne Marie to back down, to apologise, perhaps, but instead Anne Marie nodded, turned to her very best friend and told her a grown-up truth.

'Yes.'

Some mornings sped by, some mornings you didn't even get a chance to realise that the world was waking up—and some mornings you wished almost it wouldn't. And this was one of those mornings The hush on the children's ward before the drug trolley clattered past or the first of many babies woke up, that little beat of peace before the race started as Molly did her final round—looking at the babies who, despite their best efforts, ignored policy and slept on their stomachs, thumbs in, bottoms up.

And Nathan, a smile on his face and a games console in his hand as no doubt he dreamt of Bernadette and the movie he'd promised to take her to just as soon as he got out.

And Amelia… That fizz in her stomach, that funny sensation she'd felt when Anne Marie had criticised the little girl was back, only in a different form now—a sort of deep well inside that Molly was too used to. That hole, that part of her that had never been fulfilled, that had lain dry and empty, had just had a brief glimpse of the sun—this feeling, this surge, this vision of what it could be like to have a child.

A real one.

Not the baby of her dreams, but a living, breathing child.

Luke had given up with the chair and had climbed up on the bed with his daughter. His feet were dangling over the end and the two fair heads were together, his arm protectively around his child. And Molly realised it was time to close the well, to haul the cover over and block out stupid thoughts.

Maybe Anne Marie was right. Maybe she *didn't* understand what it was like to be a parent—but it was something she'd have dearly loved to have learnt. But she understood this much—Luke, her Luke, should have fixed it for his babies, should have done his damnedest anyway. The Luke she'd thought she'd known, the Luke she'd thought she'd loved would have put his children first.

Many times she'd stood at the playroom window crying quietly, watching an ambulance pull into Emergency, Security walking through the staff car park, watching the sun come up after a wretched night and trying to comprehend that the world could carry on, that no one below could possibly know the huge loss that had taken place.

And while no one had died tonight, something huge had been lost.

That little bit of hope—which she'd denied even to herself that she carried; that little bit of hope that some day, somehow, when all their cards were on the table, they might just make it.

He should have protected them—should have moved heaven and earth to keep them in a safe, happy home, whatever the cost to himself.

Two little dots, as fair and as beautiful but so

much more fragile than himself, should have been enough reason to find a way.

As blonde and as beautiful as Amanda.

The emergency nurses were out now, grabbing a quick break as they waited for an ambulance. Molly watched unseeingly the blue flash of an ambulance light as her mind whirred to an impossible place.

As blonde and beautiful as their mother.

And her head tightened at the possibility—how could she have not seen it?

Luke had had no choice but to stay.

'Molly?' His voice was as exhausted and as wretched as the man himself when she turned to face him, and her impossible question was answered. One look at him and she could see the burden he carried because Luke, *her* Luke, *would* move heaven and earth—at whatever the cost to himself. 'There's something I have to tell you…something you ought to know…'

'Don't.' She put her hand up to stop him. 'You don't have to say anything.'

'But I do,' Luke rasped, 'because I can't lose you again.'

'You could never lose me.'

'If you say the word "friend" again…' He managed a ghost of smile. 'I love you, Molly—always have, always will.'

'I love you too,' Molly said, because she did.

Good or bad, right or wrong, together or apart, she absolutely did.

'I love my kids.' He closed the door. 'I swore I'd never say this, I haven't even told Mum. But I can't lose you, Molly, not without at least giving you the truth. I don't blame you for what you think—my parents were the same, over and over they told me to leave, to get out, that she was bringing us all down. And I tried to leave. I went to a lawyer, and I was all set to go.' Molly closed her eyes at what was surely to come. 'And then she told me that they weren't…'

'I know.' Brave with his love, she looked at him, could see the confusion in his eyes—because how the hell could she know? 'I know, because I love you—and I love you because of what I know you'd do if…' Molly took a deep breath, closed her eyes and plunged into the crazy world of love. 'You don't have to say it. You never, ever have to say it.'

'They're mine!' Tears swam in those gorgeous green pools. 'I saw them being born, I held them first. If I'd left her, if I'd taken them and it had turned out she was right…'

'Have you ever…?' And she couldn't say it, couldn't demand neat, conclusive results from a DNA test for the very reasons Luke had given.

'No. Because it won't change how I feel.'

They were dancing on the periphery, and gladly so—gladly because he didn't want to say it and she didn't want to hear it—only this time it was for all the right reasons. Whatever words Amanda had hurled, be it truth or lies, whatever a blood test might prove otherwise, they were still his kids, and this beautiful, strong man had stayed—stayed for all the right reasons, even if to others they'd seemed very wrong.

'I love them first, Molly.'

And it was almost a rejection, only one that didn't sting.

'They've always come first, from the day she told me she was pregnant.'

Which was exactly how it should be—for your kids.

'I know they're wild, but they're honestly getting better. They grew up in chaos.'

'Luke, they're fabulous!' Molly halted him, because he didn't have to apologise for them. All he had to be was proud. 'They're funny and naughty and they're amazing— and they're a credit to you.'

'They will be.' Luke nodded. 'Molly, I don't need a wife, I don't need someone to run around after me. The money's starting to get sorted, and once I begin this job I can afford to get some help in.'

'I know that now.' She took a deep breath, forcing herself to be honest, hating the words she knew one day she'd have to say if she was ever going to let anyone in. 'I can't have children, Luke.'

And she waited. For what she didn't know—disappointment, perhaps, or a bit of anger that she'd lied. She finally found the courage to look up and face whatever it was going to be.

'I'm sorry,' Luke said, 'for the pain that must have caused you.'

'It did…' Molly gulped. 'It does. You don't mind?'

'Mind?' Luke frowned at her question. His voice was supremely cool, but inside his heart was pounding. Because he knew that what he said would be replayed over and over—that even if he'd got so much wrong before, this bit he had to get right. 'I mind because I love you, I mind because it's something you clearly want, but you're asking if I mind like it's some sticking point in a contract.'

'It was for Richard.' Tears tumbled out as she admitted the truth. 'He said it wasn't, of course, said that he didn't mind that I couldn't have children, but obviously he did. I'm over him.' Molly added quickly, 'Just in case you think I'm not.'

'Just not over the hurt?' Luke said, because he knew about that, and he held her, held her as if she were the most precious thing in the world. 'I wish I could give you loads of fat, happy babies—' still he held her '—because I'd give anything to make you happy.'

'But you can't.' Molly shivered. 'And one day you might—'

'Molly!' Snappy and to the point, he posed a conundrum. 'Given what I *didn't* just tell you, I don't even know if *I* can have kids!'

'Oh!'

'Does that change how you feel about me?'

'Of course not!'

He lifted her chin and looked into her eyes, could almost see the fog lifting as the truth hit home. 'So why would it change the way I feel about you? Answer the question, Molly,' he demanded when she paused in self-doubt. 'Why wouldn't it change the way I feel about you?'

'Because you love me.'

'Correct answer.' Luke nodded. 'I love you!'

As he said it he stared right into her heart, peeled off that last little piece of shell around it with his eyes. 'All of you. Even that bit of you that can't have kids. Yet somehow you work with them…' His eyes were swimming with tears now. 'And especially that bit of you that would consider loving mine.'

She really was a lousy, poor excuse for a transition girl, Molly realised, just a pathetic player at a no-strings affair, because she totally forgot to play it cool, didn't hesitate for even a second, and didn't make him sweat it out, telling him she'd get back to him. 'I love you too,' Molly answered. 'All of you…' Oh, how he'd scold later—say she wasn't a transition girl's bootlace—because she took just one very deep breath before plunging in gladly. 'All three of you!'

EPILOGUE

'THANK you!' Luke called to Amelia's departing back.

Hot and thirsty, and dressed in her very smart little school uniform, she'd demanded a drink from Molly, who, though breastfeeding a five-week-old, had pulled the angry little boy off her very sore nipple and given Amelia what she had wanted just as Luke had walked in.

'She did say thank you.' Molly winked at Amelia. 'You just didn't hear it.'

'I need something interesting for show and tell tomorrow!' Amelia frowned at her half-brother. 'But I'm not bringing *him*.'

'You're too soft,' Luke said, once Amelia had stormed out.

'She's jealous.' Molly put a very angry Hamish back on her boob and snuggled into the sofa. 'And I don't blame her a bit. I'm so lovely—why wouldn't she want all of my attention?'

'They are getting better, though.' For the hundredth time Luke picked up the end-of-year reports that had come home today. 'It's thanks to you.'

'It's thanks to us!' Molly corrected. 'And them.'

'I mean with all the changes—us, school, a new baby—you'd think they'd be more unsettled.'

They were thriving. Like two sunflowers, they just rose ever upwards, and no one could have been prouder than Molly. The feeling that had first fizzed when Amelia had had her accident bubbled over the edges now—fondness, liking, gradually growing till all it could be was love.

'I've got homework!' Angus said shyly. 'Miss Lawson said that I have to draw my family.'

'Fab!' Molly beamed, even though she was exhausted. 'Should I put lipstick on?'

'You're silly!' Angus laughed, drawing random

stick people and a big sun and a house and a tree. 'Where do I put Mum?'

'Up near the sun.' Molly smiled, but it was a very misty smile as she caught Amanda's eye.

There weren't so many photos now—loads in the kids' rooms and loads in the albums, but just one in the family room.

Which was where it should be.

She was their mum—and she'd loved them very much.

And they loved her too.

Which was how it should be.

Oh, Amanda…

As Luke ushered the twins off for bath and bed, she stared down at Hamish who, so happy to be feeding, barely flinched as two big tears plopped on his forehead.

She missed things for Amanda—so many times, so many days that Amanda should have seen and never had. The white-hot anger she'd first felt for her had now been replaced with a gentler understanding, a tolerance for others that had been a surprisingly welcome gift that helped in so many different areas of her life.

She could accept and listen and nurture the good bits about the twins' mother without barging in and judging her. And not for a single second had Molly wavered from her decision.

Molly and Luke were ready to face anything life hurled at them.

Because love ruled!

There were a fair few additions to their photo gallery. The small wedding—because it had been for both their second—hadn't, in the end, been quite so small after all.

Amelia taking centre stage as the flower girl.

Angus a very serious page boy.

And a beaming Anne Marie the Matron of honour, grinning as if she'd engineered the whole thing—which in a way she had.

Luke—well, just his usual gorgeous self, and as for Molly…

She'd looked awful!

Had wailed when the photos had come back—

at her massive stomach and pale reflection and sickly face. And for someone six months into her paediatric intensive course who was married to a doctor it was rather embarrassing really how long they'd taken to work it out.

Lying flat on her back and no doubt snoring her head off after a particularly gruelling shift, she'd woken up to Luke probing her abdomen, swearing he'd just seen something move.

'Wind,' Molly had reasoned.

'About twenty weeks' worth…' Luke had grinned.

Idiopathic.

How Bernadette had chewed over that word—how Molly had too.

Meaning no known cause…

No reason that she couldn't have children…

Till Luke had come back.

Till Luke had come back and, despite her doubts, despite being sure that you could have no such thing, finding out that she could have it all and so could he. Finding out that dreams were actually achievable when you had someone truly supporting you from the sidelines.

'Change of plan!' Luke yawned as he came back into the lounge. 'Amelia can't find her snowglobe so she's decided that she'll "make do" with Hamish.'

Taking Hamish from her, Luke smiled down at him. 'Bed!'

'It's eight o'clock!'

'And he'll be up at eleven! Come on.' He hauled her to her feet, and Molly followed, stopping at the twins' room, kissing them goodnight, nestling Hamish in his bassinet, too tired to even attempt moisturiser.

'You'll go to pot!' Molly scolded her reflection, but her reflection just shrugged and told her to replace her breast pads.

'Who are you talking to?' Luke called, lying on the bed and looking too gorgeous to be married to such a fat blob—not that you could tell, though, from the way he was looking, with *that* look as Molly crossed the room.

'No one,' Molly croaked, and did a U-turn to apply some moisturiser.

Damn!

Frantically rubbing moisturiser into her face, Molly told herself it was too soon.

Hamish was only five weeks old, for God's sake. What sort of sex maniac was she married to?

Only she'd had her check up on Wednesday and the OB had said they could try.

'Too fat!' Molly stared at the massive bosoms and tried not to think of her stomach.

Oh, God, she had sworn she'd be the perfect mother.

Tidy, organised, and back into a boxy little suit within a couple of weeks.

Not that she owned a boxy suit any more.

Grappling in the cupboard for a razor, Molly eyed with dread the boxes of condoms.

Boxes!

Multi-coloured, multi-flavoured.

'Luke!'

Luke was there in an instant, as naked as the

day he'd been born, only tall and blond—and as erect as a church steeple, which didn't really help matters.

'Six boxes!' Molly roared. 'It's a bit intimidating!'

'Oh, that!' Luke winced as the church steeple dimmed. 'I can explain. I always wondered how I'd be—you know, if I met Richard.'

'You met him?'

'At the supermarket.' He was idly playing with her big fat tummy, sort of stroking it as he spoke. 'In the medicinal aisle.'

'Oh?' He was playing with her dimply bum now, and for reasons Molly didn't even want to think about she was playing with him, raining little kisses on his nice big chest and stroking him, and even if she wasn't dressed in black and wearing some strappy little number, it felt just as good as she pictured the image of Luke bumping into her ex. 'Tell me,' Molly said, then pinched his shoulder. 'Tell me,' she urged. 'I need details.'

'She suffers from terrible migraines, apparently…'

'Bliss,' Molly whimpered, as his hand left her bottom and worked its way around.

'And what with a toddler and a baby and everything, it's a stressful time…'

'Keep going,' Molly moaned in glee.

'So I just started chucking condoms in the basket.' Luke winced. 'I know it's pathetic, but every time he reached for the paracetamol or the nasal spray I chucked another box in…' Luke flinched at his own immaturity. 'You know, to show him that I needed them and he didn't.'

'Perfect!' Molly beamed. 'I couldn't have imagined better myself.'

'Bloody embarrassing at the checkout…' Luke started, only he couldn't finish. His mind was on the same thing as Molly's.

'Hey, steady!' Luke gasped. 'Aren't I supposed to be *persuading* you?'

'Shut up,' Molly whispered, right into the shell

of his ear, back in the saddle now and rising happily to the trot. 'Just close your eyes and concentrate on us.'

MEDICAL™

Large Print

July

THE GREEK DOCTOR'S NEW-YEAR BABY	Kate Hardy
THE HEART SURGEON'S SECRET CHILD	Meredith Webber
THE MIDWIFE'S LITTLE MIRACLE	Fiona McArthur
THE SINGLE DAD'S NEW-YEAR BRIDE	Amy Andrews
THE WIFE HE'S BEEN WAITING FOR	Dianne Drake
POSH DOC CLAIMS HIS BRIDE	Anne Fraser

August

CHILDREN'S DOCTOR, SOCIETY BRIDE	Joanna Neil
THE HEART SURGEON'S BABY SURPRISE	Meredith Webber
A WIFE FOR THE BABY DOCTOR	Josie Metcalfe
THE ROYAL DOCTOR'S BRIDE	Jessica Matthews
OUTBACK DOCTOR, ENGLISH BRIDE	Leah Martyn
SURGEON BOSS, SURPRISE DAD	Janice Lynn

September

THE CHILDREN'S DOCTOR'S SPECIAL PROPOSAL	Kate Hardy
ENGLISH DOCTOR, ITALIAN BRIDE	Carol Marinelli
THE DOCTOR'S BABY BOMBSHELL	Jennifer Taylor
EMERGENCY: SINGLE DAD, MOTHER NEEDED	Laura Iding
THE DOCTOR CLAIMS HIS BRIDE	Fiona Lowe
ASSIGNMENT: BABY	Lynne Marshall

0309 LP 2P P2 Medical